Adventures in Time and Space

ADVENTURES IN TIME AND SPACE

by Frederik Pohl

TABLE OF CONTENS

THE DAY OF THE BOOMER DUKES

TABLE OF CONTENTS

FORAMINIFERA 9

Paptaste udderly, semped sempsemp dezhavoo, qued schmerz—Excuse me. I mean to say that it was like an endless diet of days, boring, tedious....

No, it loses too much in the translation. Explete my reasons, I say. Do my reasons matter? No, not to you, for you are troglodytes, knowing nothing of causes, understanding only acts. Acts and facts, I will give you acts and facts.

First you must know how I am called. My "name" is Foraminifera 9-Hart Bailey's Beam, and I am of adequate age and size. (If you doubt this, I am prepared to fight.) Once the—the tediety of life, as you might say, had made itself clear to me, there were, of course, only two alternatives. I do not like to die, so that possibility was out; and the remaining alternative was flight.

Naturally, the necessary machinery was available to me. I arrogated a small viewing machine, and scanned the centuries of the past in the hope that a sanctuary might reveal itself to my aching eyes. Kwel tediety that was! Back, back I went through the ages. Back to the Century of the Dog, back to the Age of the Crippled Men. I found no time better than my own. Back and back I peered, back as far as the Numbered Years. The Twenty-Eighth Century was boredom unendurable, the Twenty-Sixth a morass of dullness. Twenty-Fifth, Twenty-Fourth—wherever I looked, tediety was what I found.

*

I snapped off the machine and considered. Put the problem thus: Was there in all of the pages of history no age in which a 9-Hart Bailey's Beam might find adventure and excitement? There had to be! It was not possible, I told myself, despairing, that from the dawn of the dreaming primates until my own time there was no era at all in which I could be—happy? Yes, I suppose happiness is what I was looking for. But where was it? In my viewer, I had fifty centuries or more to look back upon. And that was, I decreed, the trouble; I could spend my life staring into the viewer, and yet never discover the time that was right for me. There were simply too many eras to choose from. It was like an enormous library in which there must, there had to be, contained the one fact I was looking for—that, lacking an index, I might wear my life away and never find.

"*Index!*"

I said the word aloud! For, to be sure, it was the answer. I had the freedom of the Learning Lodge, and the index in the reading room could easily find for me just what I wanted.

Splendid, splendid! I almost felt cheerful. I quickly returned the viewer I had been using to the keeper, and received my deposit back. I hurried to the Learning Lodge and fed my specifications into the index, as follows, that is to say: Find me a time in recent past where there is adventure and excitement, where there is a secret, colorful band of desperadoes with whom I can ally myself. I then added two specifications—second, that it should be before the time of the high radiation levels; and first, that it should be after the discovery of anesthesia, in case of accident—and retired to a desk in the reading room to await results.

It took only a few moments, which I occupied in making a list of the gear I wished to take with me. Then there was a hiss and a crackle, and in the receiver of the desk a book appeared. I unzipped the case, took it out, and opened it to the pages marked on the attached reading tape.

I had found my wonderland of adventure!

*

Ah, hours and days of exciting preparation! What a round of packing and buying; what a filling out of forms and a stamping of visas; what an orgy of injections and inoculations and preventive therapy! Merely getting ready for the trip made my pulse race faster and my adrenalin balance rise to the very point of paranoia; it was like being given a true blue new chance to live.

At last I was ready. I stepped into the transmission capsule; set the dials; unlocked the door, stepped out; collapsed the capsule and stored it away in my carry-all; and looked about at my new home.

Pyew! Kwel smell of staleness, of sourness, above all of coldness! It was a close matter then if I would be able to keep from a violent eructative stenosis, as you say. I closed my eyes and remembered warm violets for a moment, and then it was all right.

The coldness was not merely a smell; it was a physical fact. There was a damp grayish substance underfoot which I recognized as snow; and in a hard-surfaced roadway there were a number of wheeled vehicles moving, which caused the liquefying snow to splash about me. I adjusted my coat controls for warmth and deflection, but that was the best I could do. The reek of stale decay remained. Then there were also the buildings, painfully almost vertical. I believe it would not have disturbed me if they had been truly vertical; but many of them were minutes of arc from a true perpendicular, all of them covered with a carbonaceous material which I instantly perceived was an inadvertent deposit from the air. It was a bad beginning!

However, I was not *bored*.

*

I made my way down the "street," as you say, toward where a group of young men were walking toward me, five abreast. As I came near, they looked at me with interest and kwel respect, conversing with each other in whispers.

I addressed them: "Sirs, please direct me to the nearest recruiting office, as you call it, for the dread Camorra."

They stopped and pressed about me, looking at me intently. They were handsomely, though crudely dressed in coats of a striking orange color, and long trousers of an extremely dark material.

I decreed that I might not have made them understand me—it is always probable, it is understood, that a quicknik course in dialects of the past may not give one instant command of spoken communication in the field. I spoke again: "I wish to encounter a representative of the Camorra, in other words the Black Hand, in other words the cruel and sinister Sicilian terrorists named the Mafia. Do you know where these can be found?"

One of them said, "Nay. What's that jive?"

I puzzled over what he had said for a moment, but in the end decreed that his message was sensefree. As I was about to speak, however, he said suddenly: "Let's rove, man." And all five of them walked quickly away a few "yards." It was quite disappointing. I observed them conferring among themselves, glancing at me, and for a time proposed terminating my venture, for I then believed that it would be better to return "home," as you say, in order to more adequately research the matter.

*

However, the five young men came toward me again. The one who had spoken before, who I now detected was somewhat taller and fatter than the others, spoke as follows: "You're wanting the Mafia?" I agreed. He looked at me for a moment. "Are you holding?"

He was inordinately hard to understand. I said, slowly and with patience, "Keska that 'holding' say?"

"Money, man. You going to slip us something to help you find these cats?"

"Certainly, money. I have a great quantity of money instantly available," I rejoined him. This appeared to relieve his mind.

There was a short pause, directly after which this first of the young men spoke: "You're on, man. Yeah, come with us. What's to call you?" I queried this last statement, and he expanded: "The name. What's the name?"

"You may call me Foraminifera 9," I directed, since I wished to be incognito, as you put it, and we proceeded along the "street." All five of the young men indicated a desire to serve me, offering indeed to take my carry-all. I rejected this, politely.

I looked about me with lively interest, as you may well believe. Kwel dirt, kwel dinginess, kwel cold! And yet there was a certain charm which I can determine no way of expressing in this language. Acts and facts, of course. I shall not attempt to capture the subjectivity which is the charm, only to transcribe the physical datum—perhaps even data, who knows? My companions, for example: They were in appearance overwrought, looking about them continually, stopping entirely and drawing me with them into the shelter of a "door" when another man, this one wearing blue clothing and a visored hat appeared. Yet they were clearly devoted to me, at that moment, since they had put aside their own projects in order to escort me without delay to the Mafia.

*

Mafia! Fortunate that I had found them to lead me to the Mafia! For it had been clear in the historical work I had consulted that it was not ultimately easy to gain access to the Mafia. Indeed, so secret were they that I had detected no trace of their existence in other histories of the period. Had I relied only on the conventional work, I might never have known of their great underground struggle against what you term society. It was only in the actual contemporary volume itself, the curiosity titled U.S.A. Confidential by one Lait and one Mortimer, that I had descried that, throughout the world, this great revolutionary organization flexed its tentacles, the plexus within a short distance of where I now stood, battling courageously. With me to help them, what heights might we not attain! Kwel dramatic delight!

My meditations were interrupted. "Boomers!" asserted one of my five escorts in a loud, frightened tone. "Let's cut, man!" he continued, leading me with them into another entrance. It appeared, as well as I could decree, that the cause of his ejaculative outcry was the discovery of perhaps three, perhaps four, other young men, in coats of the same shiny material as my escorts. The difference was that they were of a different color, being blue.

*

We hastened along a lengthy chamber which was quite dark, immediately after which the large, heavy one opened a way to a serrated incline leading downward. It was extremely dark, I should say. There was also an extreme smell, quite like that of the outer air, but enormously intensified; one would suspect that there was an incomplete combustion of, perhaps, wood or coal, as well as a certain quantity of general decay. At any rate, we reached the bottom of the incline, and my escort behaved quite badly. One of them said to the other four, in these words: "Them jumpers follow us sure. Yeah, there's much trouble. What's to prime this guy now and split?"

Instantly they fell upon me with violence. I had fortunately become rather alarmed at their visible emotion of fear, and already had taken from my carry-all a Stollgratz 16, so that I quickly turned it on them. I started to replace the Stollgratz 16 as they fell to the floor, yet I realized that there might be an additional element of danger. Instead of putting the Stollgratz 16 in with the other trade goods, which I had brought to assist me in negotiating with the Mafia, I transferred it to my jacket. It had become clear to me that the five young men of my escort had intended to abduct and rob me—indeed had intended it all along, perhaps having never intended to convoy me to the office of the Mafia. And the other young men, those who wore the blue jackets in place of the orange, were already descending the incline toward me, quite rapidly.

"Stop," I directed them. "I shall not entrust myself to you until you have given me evidence that you entirely deserve such trust."

*

They all halted, regarding me and the Stollgratz 16. I detected that one of them said to another: "That cat's got a zip."

The other denied this, saying: "That no zip, man. Yeah, look at them Leopards. Say, you bust them flunkies with that thing?"

I perceived his meaning quite quickly. "You are 'correct'," I rejoined. "Are you associated in friendship with them flunkies?"

"Hell, no. Yeah, they're Leopards and we're Boomer Dukes. You cool them, you do us much good." I received this information as indicating that the two socio-economic units were inimical, and unfortunately lapsed into an example of the Bivalent Error. Since p implied not-q, I sloppily assumed that not-q implied r (with, you understand, r being taken as the class of phenomena pertinently favorable to me). This was a very poor construction, and of course resulted in certain difficulties. Qued, after all. I stated:

"Them flunkies offered to conduct me to a recruiting office, as you say, of the Mafia, but instead tried to take from me the much money I am holding." I then went on to describe to them my desire to attain contact with the said Mafia; meanwhile they descended further and grouped about me in the very little light, examining curiously the motionless figures of the Leopards.

They seemed to be greatly impressed; and at the same time, very much puzzled. Naturally. They looked at the Leopards, and then at me.

They gave every evidence of wishing to help me; but of course if I had not forgotten that one cannot assume from the statements "not-Leopard implies Boomer Duke" and "not-Leopard implies Foraminifera 9" that, qued, "Boomer Duke implies Foraminifera 9" ... if I had not forgotten this, I say, I should not have been "deceived." For in practice they were as little favorable to me as the Leopards. A certain member of their party reached a position behind me.

I quickly perceived that his intention was not favorable, and attempted to turn around in order to discharge at him with the Stollgratz 16, but he was very rapid. He had a metallic cylinder, and with it struck my head, knocking "me" unconscious.

SHIELD 8805

This candy store is called Chris's. There must be ten thousand like it in the city. A marble counter with perhaps five stools, a display case of cigars and a bigger one of candy, a few dozen girlie magazines hanging by clothespin-sort-of things from wire ropes along the wall. It has a couple of very small glass-topped tables under the magazines. And a juke—I can't imagine a place like Chris's without a juke.

I had been sitting around Chris's for a couple of hours, and I was beginning to get edgy. The reason I was sitting around Chris's was not that I liked Cokes particularly, but that it was one of the hanging-out places of a juvenile gang called The Leopards, with whom I had been trying to work for nearly a year; and the reason I was becoming edgy was that I didn't see any of them there.

The boy behind the counter—he had the same first name as I, Walter in both cases, though my last name is Hutner and his is, I believe, something Puerto Rican—the boy behind the counter was dummying up, too. I tried to talk to him, on and off, when he wasn't busy. He wasn't busy most of the time; it was too cold for sodas. But he just didn't want to talk. Now, these kids love to talk. A lot of what they say doesn't make sense—either bullying, or bragging, or purposeless swearing—but talk is their normal state; when they quiet down it means trouble. For instance, if you ever find yourself walking down Thirty-Fifth Street and a couple of kids pass you, talking, you don't have to bother looking around; but if they stop talking, turn quickly. You're about to be mugged. Not that Walt was a mugger—as far as I know; but that's the pattern of the enclave.

*

So his being quiet was a bad sign. It might mean that a rumble was brewing—and that meant that my work so far had been pretty nearly a failure. Even worse, it might mean that somehow the Leopards had discovered that I had at last passed my examinations and been appointed to the New York City Police Force as a rookie patrolman, Shield 8805.

Trying to work with these kids is hard enough at best. They don't like outsiders. But they particularly hate cops, and I had been trying for some weeks to decide how I could break the news to them.

The door opened. Hawk stood there. He didn't look at me, which was a bad sign. Hawk was one of the youngest in the Leopards, a skinny, very dark kid who had been reasonably friendly to me. He stood in the open door, with snow blowing in past him. "Walt. Out here, man."

It wasn't me he meant—they call me "Champ," I suppose because I beat them all shooting eight-ball pool. Walt put down the comic he had been reading and walked out, also without looking at me. They closed the door.

*

Time passed. I saw them through the window, talking to each other, looking at me. It was something, all right. They were scared. That's bad, because these kids are like wild animals; if you scare them, they hit first—it's the only way they know to defend themselves. But on the other hand, a rumble wouldn't scare them—not where they would show it; and finding out about the shield in my pocket wouldn't scare them, either. They hated cops, as I say; but cops were a part of their environment. It was strange, and baffling.

Walt came back in, and Hawk walked rapidly away. Walt went behind the counter, lit a cigaret, wiped at the marble top, picked up his comic, put it down again and finally looked at me. He said: "Some punk busted Fayo and a couple of the boys. It's real trouble."

I didn't say anything.

He took a puff on his cigaret. "They're chilled, Champ. Five of them."

"Chilled? Dead?" It sounded bad; there hadn't been a real rumble in months, not with a killing.

He shook his head. "Not dead. You're wanting to see, you go down Gomez's cellar. Yeah, they're all stiff but they're breathing. I be along soon as the old man comes back in the store."

He looked pretty sick. I left it at that and hurried down the block to the tenement where the Gomez family lived, and then I found out why.

*

They were sprawled on the filthy floor of the cellar like winoes in an alley. Fayo, who ran the gang; Jap; Baker; two others I didn't know as well. They were breathing, as Walt had said, but you just couldn't wake them up.

Hawk and his twin brother, Yogi, were there with them, looking scared. I couldn't blame them. The kids looked perfectly all right, but it was obvious that they weren't. I bent down and smelled, but there was no trace of liquor or anything else on their breath.

I stood up. "We'd better get a doctor."

"Nay. You call the meat wagon, and a cop comes right with it, man," Yogi said, and his brother nodded.

I laid off that for a moment. "What happened?"

Hawk said, "You know that witch Gloria, goes with one of the Boomer Dukes? She opened her big mouth to my girl. Yeah, opened her mouth and much bad talk came out. Said Fayo primed some jumper with a zip and the punk cooled him, and then a couple of the Boomers moved in real cool. Now they got the punk with the zip and much other stuff, real stuff."

"What kind of stuff?"

Hawk looked worried. He finally admitted that he didn't know what kind of stuff, but it was something dangerous in the way of weapons. It had been the "zip" that had knocked out the five Leopards.

I sent Hawk out to the drug-store for smelling salts and containers of hot black coffee—not that I knew what I was doing, of course, but they were dead set against calling an ambulance. And the boys didn't seem to be in any particular danger, only sleep.

*

However, even then I knew that this kind of trouble was something I couldn't handle alone. It was a tossup what to do—the smart thing was to call the precinct right then and there; but I couldn't help feeling that that would make the Leopards clam up hopelessly. The six months I had spent trying to work with them had not been too successful—a lot of the other neighborhood workers had made a lot more progress than I—but at least they were willing to talk to me; and they wouldn't talk to uniformed police.

Besides, as soon as I had been sworn in, the day before, I had begun the practice of carrying my .38 at all times, as the regulations say. It was in my coat. There was no reason for me to feel I needed it. But I did. If there was any truth to the story of a "zip" knocking out the boys—and I had all five of them right there for evidence—I had the unpleasant conviction that there was real trouble circulating around East Harlem that afternoon.

"Champ. They all waking up!"

I turned around, and Hawk was right. The five Leopards, all of a sudden, were stirring and opening their eyes. Maybe the smelling salts had something to do with it, but I rather think not.

We fed them some of the black coffee, still reasonably hot. They were scared; they were more scared than anything I had ever seen in those kids before. They could hardly talk at first, and when finally they came around enough to tell me what had happened I could hardly believe them. This man had been small and peculiar, and he had been looking for, of all things, the "Mafia," which he had read about in history books—*old* history books.

Well, it didn't make sense, unless you were prepared to make a certain assumption that I refused to make. Man from Mars? Nonsense. Or from the future? Equally ridiculous....

*

Then the five Leopards, reviving, began to walk around. The cellar was dark and dirty, and packed with the accumulation of generations in the way of old furniture and rat-inhabited mattresses and piles of newspapers; it wasn't surprising that we hadn't noticed the little gleaming thing that had apparently rolled under an abandoned potbelly stove.

Jap picked it up, squalled, dropped it and yelled for me.

I touched it cautiously, and it tingled. It wasn't painful, but it was an odd, unexpected feeling—perhaps you've come across the "buzzers" that novelty stores sell which, concealed in the palm, give a sudden, surprising tingle when the owner shakes hands with an unsuspecting friend. It was like that, like a mild electric shock. I picked it up and held it. It gleamed brightly, with a light of its own; it was round; it made a faint droning sound; I turned it over, and it spoke to me. It said in a friendly, feminine whisper: *Warning, this portatron attuned only to Bailey's Beam percepts. Remain quiescent until the Adjuster comes.*

That settled it. Any time a lit-up cue ball talks to me, I refer the matter to higher authority. I decided on the spot that I was heading for the precinct house, no matter what the Leopards thought.

But when I turned and headed for the stairs, I couldn't move. My feet simply would not lift off the ground. I twisted, and stumbled, and fell in a heap; I yelled for help, but it didn't do any good. The Leopards couldn't move either.

We were stuck there in Gomez's cellar, as though we had been nailed to the filthy floor.

COW

When I see what this flunky has done to them Leopards, I call him a cool cat right away. But then we jump him and he ain't so cool. Angel and Tiny grab him under the arms and I'm grabbing the stuff he's carrying. Yeah, we get out of there.

There's bulls on the street, so we cut through the back and over the fences. Tiny don't like that. He tells me, "Cow. What's to leave this cat here? He must weigh eighteen tons." "You're bringing him," I tell him, so he shuts up. That's how it is in the Boomer Dukes. When Cow talks, them other flunkies shut up fast.

We get him in the loft over the R. and I. Social Club. Damn, but it's cold up there. I can hear the pool balls clicking down below so I pass the word to keep quiet. Then I give this guy the foot and pretty soon he wakes up.

As soon as I talk to him a little bit I figure we had luck riding with us when we see them Leopards. This cat's got real bad stuff. Yeah, I never hear of anything like it. But what it takes to make a fight he's got. I take my old pistol and give it to Tiny. Hell, it makes him happy and what's it cost me? Because what this cat's got makes that pistol look like something for babies.

*

First he don't want to talk. "Stomp him," I tell Angel, but he's scared. He says, "Nay. This is a real weird cat, Cow. I'm for cutting out of here."

"Stomp him," I tell him again, pretty quiet, but he does it. He don't have to tell me this cat's weird, but when the cat gets the foot a couple of times he's willing to talk. Yeah, he talks real funny, but that don't matter to me. We take all the loot out of his bag, and I make this cat tell me what it's to do. Damn, I don't know what he's talking about one time out of six, but I know enough. Even Tiny catches on after a while, because I see him put down that funky old pistol I gave him that he's been loving up.

I'm feeling pretty good. I wish a couple of them chicken Leopards would turn up so I could show them what they missed out on. Yeah, I'll take on them, and the Black Dogs, and all the cops in the world all at once—that's how good I'm feeling. I feel so good that I don't even like it when Angel lets out a yell and comes up with a wad of loot. It's like I want to prime the U.S. Mint for chickenfeed, I don't want it to come so easy.

But money's on hand, so I take it off Angel and count it. This cat was really loaded; there must be a thousand dollars here.

I take a handful of it and hand it over to Angel real cool. "Get us some charge," I tell him. "There's much to do and I'm feeling ready for some charge to do it with."

"How many sticks you want me to get?" he asks, holding on to that money like he never saw any before.

I tell him: "Sticks? Nay. I'm for real stuff tonight. You find Four-Eye and get us some horse." Yeah, he digs me then. He looks like he's pretty scared and I know he is, because this punk hasn't had anything bigger than reefers in his life. But I'm for busting a couple of caps of H, and what I do he's going to do. He takes off to find Four-Eye and the rest of us get busy on this cat with the funny artillery until he gets back.

*

It's like I'm a million miles down Dream Street. Hell, I don't want to wake up.

But the H is wearing off and I'm feeling mean. Damn, I'll stomp my mother if she talks big to me right then.

I'm the first one on my feet and I'm looking for trouble. The whole place is full now. Angel must have passed the word to everybody in the Dukes, but I don't even remember them coming in. There's eight or ten cats lying around on the floor now, not even moving. This won't do, I decide.

If I'm on my feet, they're all going to be on their feet. I start to give them the foot and they begin to move. Even the weirdie must've had some H. I'm guessing that somebody slipped him some to see what would happen, because he's off on Cloud Number Nine. Yeah, they're feeling real mean when they wake up, but I handle them cool. Even that little flunky Sailor starts to go up against me but I look at him cool and he chickens. Angel and Pete are real sick, with the shakes and the heaves, but I ain't waiting for them to feel good. "Give me that loot," I tell Tiny, and he hands over the stuff we took off the weirdie. I start to pass out the stuff.

"What's to do with this stuff?" Tiny asks me, looking at what I'm giving him.

I tell him, "Point it and shoot it." He isn't listening when the weirdie's telling me what the stuff is. He wants to know what it does, but I don't know that. I just tell him, "Point it and shoot it, man." I've sent one of the cats out for drinks and smokes and he's back by then, and we're all beginning to feel a little better, only still pretty mean. They begin to dig me.

"Yeah, it sounds like a rumble," one of them says, after a while.

I give him the nod, cool. "You're calling it," I tell him. "There's much fighting tonight. The Boomer Dukes is taking on the world!"

SANDY VAN PELT

The front office thought the radio car would give us a break in spot news coverage, and I guessed as wrong as they did. I had been covering City Hall long enough, and that's no place to build a career—the Press Association is very tight there, there's not much chance of getting any kind of exclusive story because of the sharing agreements. So I put in for the radio car. It meant taking the night shift, but I got it.

I suppose the front office got their money's worth, because they played up every lousy auto smash the radio car covered as though it were the story of the Second Coming, and maybe it helped circulation. But I had been on it for four months and, wouldn't you know it, there wasn't a decent murder, or sewer explosion, or running gun fight between six P.M. and six A.M. any night I was on duty in those whole four months. What made it worse, the kid they gave me as photographer—Sol Detweiler, his name was—couldn't drive worth a damn, so I was stuck with chauffeuring us around.

We had just been out to LaGuardia to see if it was true that Marilyn Monroe was sneaking into town with Aly Khan on a night plane—it wasn't—and we were coming across the Triborough Bridge, heading south toward the East River Drive, when the office called. I pulled over and parked and answered the radiophone.

*

It was Harrison, the night City Editor. "Listen, Sandy, there's a gang fight in East Harlem. Where are you now?"

It didn't sound like much to me, I admit. "There's always a gang fight in East Harlem, Harrison. I'm cold and I'm on my way down to Night Court, where there may or may not be a story; but at least I can get my feet warm."

"*Where are you now?*" Harrison wasn't fooling. I looked at Sol, on the seat next to me; I thought I had heard him snicker. He began to fiddle with his camera without looking at me. I pushed the "talk" button and told Harrison where I was. It pleased him very much; I wasn't more than six blocks from where this big rumble was going on, he told me, and he made it very clear that I was to get on over there immediately.

I pulled away from the curb, wondering why I had ever wanted to be a newspaperman; I could have made five times as much money for half as much work in an ad agency. To make it worse, I heard Sol chuckle again. The reason he was so amused was that when we first teamed up I made the mistake of telling him what a hot reporter I was, and I had been visibly cooling off before his eyes for a better than four straight months.

Believe me, I was at the very bottom of my career that night. For five cents cash I would have parked the car, thrown the keys in the East River, and taken the first bus out of town. I was absolutely positive that the story would be a bust and all I would get out of it would be a bad cold from walking around in the snow.

And if that doesn't show you what a hot newspaperman I really am, nothing will.

*

Sol began to act interested as we reached the corner Harrison had told us to go to. "That's Chris's," he said, pointing at a little candy store. "And that must be the pool hall where the Leopards hang out."

"You know this place?"

He nodded. "I know a man named Walter Hutner. He and I went to school together, until he dropped out, couple weeks ago. He quit college to go to the Police Academy. He wanted to be a cop."

I looked at him. "You're going to college?"

"Sure, Mr. Van Pelt. Wally Hutner was a sociology major—I'm journalism—but we had a couple of classes together. He had a part-time job with a neighborhood council up here, acting as a sort of adult adviser for one of the gangs."

"They need advice on how to be gangs?"

"No, that's not it, Mr. Van Pelt. The councils try to get their workers accepted enough to bring the kids in to the social centers, that's all. They try to get them off the streets. Wally was working with a bunch called the Leopards."

I shut him up. "Tell me about it later!" I stopped the car and rolled down a window, listening.

*

Yes, there was something going on all right. Not at the corner Harrison had mentioned—there wasn't a soul in sight in any direction. But I could hear what sounded like gunfire and yelling, and, my God, even bombs going off! And it wasn't too far away. There were sirens, too—squad cars, no doubt.

"It's over that way!" Sol yelled, pointing. He looked as though he was having the time of his life, all keyed up and delighted. He didn't have to tell me where the noise was coming from, I could hear for myself. It sounded like D-Day at Normandy, and I didn't like the sound of it.

I made a quick decision and slammed on the brakes, then backed the car back the way we had come. Sol looked at me. "What—"

"Local color," I explained quickly. "This the place you were talking about? Chris's? Let's go in and see if we can find some of these hoodlums."

"But, Mr. Van Pelt, all the pictures are over where the fight's going on!"

"Pictures, shmictures! Come on!" I got out in front of the candy store, and the only thing he could do was follow me.

Whatever they were doing, they were making the devil's own racket about it. Now that I looked a little more closely I could see that they must have come this way; the candy store's windows were broken; every other street light was smashed; and what had at first looked like a flight of steps in front of a tenement across the street wasn't anything of the kind—it was a pile of bricks and stone from the false-front cornice on the roof! How in the world they had managed to knock that down I had no idea; but it sort of convinced me that, after all, Harrison had been right about this being a *big* fight. Over where the noise was coming from there were queer flashing lights in the clouds overhead—reflecting exploding flares, I thought.

*

No, I didn't want to go over where the pictures were. I like living. If it had been a normal Harlem rumble with broken bottles and knives, or maybe even home-made zip guns—I might have taken a chance on it, but this was for real.

"Come on," I yelled to Sol, and we pushed the door open to the candy store.

At first there didn't seem to be anyone in, but after we called a couple times a kid of about sixteen, coffee-colored and scared-looking, stuck his head up above the counter.

"You. What's going on here?" I demanded. He looked at me as if I was some kind of a two-headed monster. "Come on, kid. Tell us what happened."

"Excuse me, Mr. Van Pelt." Sol cut in ahead of me and began talking to the kid in Spanish. It got a rise out of him; at least Sol got an answer. My Spanish is only a little bit better than my Swahili, so I missed what was going on, except for an occasional word. But Sol was getting it all. He reported: "He knows Walt; that's what's bothering him. He says Walt and some of the Leopards are in a basement down the street, and there's something wrong with them. I can't exactly figure out what, but—"

"The hell with them. What about *that?*"

"You mean the fight? Oh, it's a big one all right, Mr. Van Pelt. It's a gang called the Boomer Dukes. They've got hold of some real guns somewhere—I can't exactly understand what kind of guns he means, but it sounds like something serious. He says they shot that parapet down across the street. Gosh, Mr. Van Pelt, you'd think it'd take a cannon for something like that. But it has something to do with Walt Hutner and all the Leopards, too."

I said enthusiastically, "Very good, Sol. That's fine. Find out where the cellar is, and we'll go interview Hutner."

"But Mr. Van Pelt, the pictures—"

"Sorry. I have to call the office." I turned my back on him and headed for the car.

*

The noise was louder, and the flashes in the sky brighter—it looked as though they were moving this way. Well, I didn't have any money tied up in the car, so I wasn't worried about leaving it in the street. And somebody's cellar seemed like a very good place to be. I called the office and started to tell Harrison what we'd found out; but he stopped me short. "Sandy, where've you been? I've been trying to call you for—Listen, we got a call from Fordham. They've detected radiation coming from the East Side—it's got to be what's going on up there! Radiation, do you hear me? That means atomic weapons! Now, you get th—"

Silence.

"Hello?" I cried, and then remembered to push the talk button. "Hello? Harrison, you there?"

Silence. The two-way radio was dead.

I got out of the car; and maybe I understood what had happened to the radio and maybe I didn't. Anyway, there was something new shining in the sky. It hung below the clouds in parts, and I could see it through the bottom of the clouds in the middle; it was a silvery teacup upside down, a hemisphere over everything.

It hadn't been there two minutes before.

*

I heard firing coming closer and closer. Around a corner a bunch of cops came, running, turning, firing; running, turning and firing again. It was like the retreat from Caporetto in miniature. And what was chasing them? In a minute I saw. Coming around the corner was a kid with a lightning-blue satin jacket and two funny-looking guns in his hand; there was a silvery aura around him, the same color as the lights in the sky; and I swear I saw those cops' guns hit him twenty times in twenty seconds, but he didn't seem to notice.

Sol and the kid from the candy store were right beside me. We took another look at the one-man army that was coming down the street toward us, laughing and prancing and firing those odd-looking guns. And then the three of us got out of there, heading for the cellar. Any cellar.

PRIAM'S MAW

My occupation was "short-order cook", as it is called. I practiced it in a locus entitled "The White Heaven," established at Fifth Avenue, Newyork, between 1949 and 1962 C.E. I had created rapport with several of the aboriginals, who addressed me as Bessie, and presumed to approve the manner in which I heated specimens of minced ruminant quadruped flesh (deceased to be sure). It was a satisfactory guise, although tiring.

Using approved techniques, I was compiling anthropometric data while "I" was, as they say, "brewing coffee." I deem the probability nearly conclusive that it was the double duty, plus the datum that, as stated, "I" was physically tired, which caused me to overlook the first signal from my portatron. Indeed, I might have overlooked the second as well except that the aboriginal named Lester stated: "Hey, Bessie. Ya got an alarm clock in ya pocketbook?" He had related the annunciator signal of the portatron to the only significant datum in his own experience which it resembled, the ringing of a bell.

I annotated his dossier to provide for his removal in case it eventuated that he had made an undesirable intuit (this proved unnecessary) and retired to the back of the "store" with my carry-all. On identifying myself to the portatron, I received information that it was attuned to a Bailey's Beam, identified as Foraminifera 9-Hart, who had refused treatment for systemic weltschmerz and instead sought to relieve his boredom by adventuring into this era.

I thereupon compiled two recommendations which are attached: 2, a proposal for reprimand to the Keeper of the Learning Lodge for failure to properly annotate a volume entitled U.S.A. Confidential and, 1, a proposal for reprimand to the Transport Executive, for permitting Bailey's Beam-class personnel access to temporal transport. Meanwhile, I left the "store" by a rear exit and directed myself toward the locus of the transmitting portatron.

*

I had proximately left when I received an additional information, namely that developed weapons were being employed in the area toward which I was directing. This provoked that I abandon guise entirely. I went transparent and quickly examined all aboriginals within view, to determine if any required removal; but none had observed this. I rose to perhaps seventy-five meters and sped at full atmospheric driving speed toward the source of the alarm. As I crossed a "park" I detected the drive of another Adjuster, whom I determined to be Alephplex Priam's Maw—that is, my father. He bespoke me as follows: "Hurry, Besplex Priam's Maw. That crazy Foraminifera has been captured by aboriginals and they have taken his weapons away from him." "Weapons?" I inquired. "Yes, weapons," he stated, "for Foraminifera 9-Hart brought with him more than forty-three kilograms of weapons, ranging up to and including electronic."

I recorded this datum and we landed, went opaque in the shelter of a doorway and examined our percepts. "Quarantine?" asked my father, and I had to agree. "Quarantine," I voted, and he opened his carry-all and set-up a quarantine shield on the console. At once appeared the silvery quarantine dome, and the first step of our adjustment was completed. Now to isolate, remove, replace.

Queried Alephplex: "An Adjuster?" I observed the phenomenon to which he was referring. A young, dark aboriginal was coming toward us on the "street," driving a group of police aboriginals before him. He was armed, it appeared, with a fission-throwing weapon in one hand and some sort of tranquilizer—I deem it to have been a Stollgratz 16—in the other; moreover, he wore an invulnerability belt. The police aboriginals were attempting to strike him with missile weapons, which the belt deflected. I neutralized his shield, collapsed him and stored him in my carry-all. "Not an Adjuster," I asserted my father, but he had already perceived that this was so. I left him to neutralize and collapse the police aboriginals while I zeroed in on the portatron. I did not envy him his job with the police aboriginals, for many of them were "dead," as they say. It required the most delicate adjustments.

*

The portatron developed to be in a "cellar" and with it were some nine or eleven aboriginals which it had immobilized pending my arrival. One spoke to me thus: "Young lady, please call the cops! We're stuck here, and—" I did not wait to hear what he wished to say further, but neutralized and collapsed him with the other aboriginals. The portatron apologized for having caused me inconvenience; but of course it was not its fault, so I did not neutralize it. Using it for d-f, I quickly located the culprit, Foraminifera 9-Hart Bailey's Beam, nearby. He spoke despairingly in the dialect of the locus, "Besplex Priam's Maw, for God's sake get me out of this!" "Out!" I spoke to him, "you'll wish you never were 'born,' as they say!" I neutralized but did not collapse him, pending instructions from the Central Authority. The aboriginals who were with him, however, I did collapse.

Presently arrived Alephplex, along with four other Adjusters who had arrived before the quarantine shield made it not possible for anyone else to enter the disturbed area. Each one of us had had to abandon guise, so that this locus of Newyork 1939-1986 must require new Adjusters to replace us—a matter to be charged against the guilt of Foraminifera 9-Hart Bailey's Beam, I deem.

*

This concluded Steps 3 and 2 of our Adjustment, the removal and the isolation of the disturbed specimens. We are transmitting same disturbed specimens to you under separate cover herewith, in neutralized and collapsed state, for the manufacture of simulacra thereof. One regrets to say that they number three thousand eight hundred forty-six, comprising all aboriginals within the quarantined

area who had first-hand knowledge of the anachronisms caused by
Foraminifera's importation of contemporary weapons into this locus.

Alephplex and the four other Adjusters are at present
reconstructing such physical damage as was caused by the use of said
weapons. Simultaneously, while I am preparing this report, "I" am
maintaining the quarantine shield which cuts off this locus, both
physically and temporally, from the remainder of its environment. I
deem that if replacements for the attached aboriginals can be
fabricated quickly enough, there will be no significant outside percept
of the shield itself, or of the happenings within it—that is, by
maintaining a quasi-stasis of time while the repairs are being made,
an outside aboriginal observer will see, at most, a mere flicker of
silver in the sky. All Adjusters here present are working as rapidly as
we can to make sure the shield can be withdrawn, before so many
aboriginals have observed it as to make it necessary to replace the
entire city with simulacra. We do not wish a repetition of the
California incident, after all.

THE TUNNEL UNDER THE WORLD

TABLE OF CONTENTS

I

On the morning of June 15th, Guy Burckhardt woke up screaming out of a dream.

It was more real than any dream he had ever had in his life. He could still hear and feel the sharp, ripping-metal explosion, the violent heave that had tossed him furiously out of bed, the searing wave of heat.

He sat up convulsively and stared, not believing what he saw, at the quiet room and the bright sunlight coming in the window.

He croaked, "Mary?"

His wife was not in the bed next to him. The covers were tumbled and awry, as though she had just left it, and the memory of the dream was so strong that instinctively he found himself searching the floor to see if the dream explosion had thrown her down.

But she wasn't there. Of course she wasn't, he told himself, looking at the familiar vanity and slipper chair, the uncracked window, the unbuckled wall. It had only been a dream.

"Guy?" His wife was calling him querulously from the foot of the stairs. "Guy, dear, are you all right?"

He called weakly, "Sure."

There was a pause. Then Mary said doubtfully, "Breakfast is ready. Are you sure you're all right? I thought I heard you yelling—"

Burckhardt said more confidently, "I had a bad dream, honey. Be right down."

*

In the shower, punching the lukewarm-and-cologne he favored, he told himself that it had been a beaut of a dream. Still, bad dreams weren't unusual, especially bad dreams about explosions. In the past thirty years of H-bomb jitters, who had not dreamed of explosions?

Even Mary had dreamed of them, it turned out, for he started to tell her about the dream, but she cut him off. "You *did?*" Her voice was astonished. "Why, dear, I dreamed the same thing! Well, almost the same thing. I didn't actually *hear* anything. I dreamed that something woke me up, and then there was a sort of quick bang, and then something hit me on the head. And that was all. Was yours like that?"

Burckhardt coughed. "Well, no," he said. Mary was not one of these strong-as-a-man, brave-as-a-tiger women. It was not necessary, he thought, to tell her all the little details of the dream that made it seem so real. No need to mention the splintered ribs, and the salt bubble in his throat, and the agonized knowledge that this was death. He said, "Maybe there really was some kind of explosion downtown. Maybe we heard it and it started us dreaming."

Mary reached over and patted his hand absently. "Maybe," she agreed. "It's almost half-past eight, dear. Shouldn't you hurry? You don't want to be late to the office."

He gulped his food, kissed her and rushed out—not so much to be on time as to see if his guess had been right.

But downtown Tylerton looked as it always had. Coming in on the bus, Burckhardt watched critically out the window, seeking evidence of an explosion. There wasn't any. If anything, Tylerton looked better than it ever had before: It was a beautiful crisp day, the sky was cloudless, the buildings were clean and inviting. They had, he observed, steam-blasted the Power & Light Building, the town's only skyscraper—that was the penalty of having Contro Chemical's main plant on the outskirts of town; the fumes from the cascade stills left their mark on stone buildings.

None of the usual crowd were on the bus, so there wasn't anyone Burckhardt could ask about the explosion. And by the time he got out at the corner of Fifth and Lehigh and the bus rolled away with a muted diesel moan, he had pretty well convinced himself that it was all imagination.

He stopped at the cigar stand in the lobby of his office building, but Ralph wasn't behind the counter. The man who sold him his pack of cigarettes was a stranger.

"Where's Mr. Stebbins?" Burckhardt asked.

The man said politely, "Sick, sir. He'll be in tomorrow. A pack of Marlins today?"

"Chesterfields," Burckhardt corrected.

"Certainly, sir," the man said. But what he took from the rack and slid across the counter was an unfamiliar green-and-yellow pack.

"Do try these, sir," he suggested. "They contain an anti-cough factor. Ever notice how ordinary cigarettes make you choke every once in a while?"

*

Burckhardt said suspiciously, "I never heard of this brand."

"Of course not. They're something new." Burckhardt hesitated, and the man said persuasively, "Look, try them out at my risk. If you don't like them, bring back the empty pack and I'll refund your money. Fair enough?"

Burckhardt shrugged. "How can I lose? But give me a pack of Chesterfields, too, will you?"

He opened the pack and lit one while he waited for the elevator. They weren't bad, he decided, though he was suspicious of cigarettes that had the tobacco chemically treated in any way. But he didn't think much of Ralph's stand-in; it would raise hell with the trade at the cigar stand if the man tried to give every customer the same high-pressure sales talk.

The elevator door opened with a low-pitched sound of music. Burckhardt and two or three others got in and he nodded to them as the door closed. The thread of music switched off and the speaker in the ceiling of the cab began its usual commercials.

No, not the *usual* commercials, Burckhardt realized. He had been exposed to the captive-audience commercials so long that they hardly registered on the outer ear any more, but what was coming from the recorded program in the basement of the building caught his attention. It wasn't merely that the brands were mostly unfamiliar; it was a difference in pattern.

There were jingles with an insistent, bouncy rhythm, about soft drinks he had never tasted. There was a rapid patter dialogue between what sounded like two ten-year-old boys about a candy bar, followed by an authoritative bass rumble: "Go right out and get a DELICIOUS Choco-Bite and eat your TANGY Choco-Bite *all up*. That's *Choco-Bite*!" There was a sobbing female whine: "I *wish* I had a Feckle Freezer! I'd do *anything* for a Feckle Freezer!" Burckhardt reached his floor and left the elevator in the middle of the last one. It left him a little uneasy. The commercials were not for familiar brands; there was no feeling of use and custom to them.

But the office was happily normal—except that Mr. Barth wasn't in. Miss Mitkin, yawning at the reception desk, didn't know exactly why. "His home phoned, that's all. He'll be in tomorrow."

"Maybe he went to the plant. It's right near his house."

She looked indifferent. "Yeah."

A thought struck Burckhardt. "But today is June 15th! It's quarterly tax return day—he has to sign the return!"

Miss Mitkin shrugged to indicate that that was Burckhardt's problem, not hers. She returned to her nails.

Thoroughly exasperated, Burckhardt went to his desk. It wasn't that he couldn't sign the tax returns as well as Barth, he thought resentfully. It simply wasn't his job, that was all; it was a responsibility that Barth, as office manager for Contro Chemicals' downtown office, should have taken.

*

He thought briefly of calling Barth at his home or trying to reach him at the factory, but he gave up the idea quickly enough. He didn't really care much for the people at the factory and the less contact he had with them, the better. He had been to the factory once, with Barth; it had been a confusing and, in a way, a frightening experience. Barring a handful of executives and engineers, there wasn't a soul in the factory—that is, Burckhardt corrected himself, remembering what Barth had told him, not a *living* soul—just the machines.

According to Barth, each machine was controlled by a sort of computer which reproduced, in its electronic snarl, the actual memory and mind of a human being. It was an unpleasant thought. Barth, laughing, had assured him that there was no Frankenstein business of robbing graveyards and implanting brains in machines. It was only a matter, he said, of transferring a man's habit patterns from brain cells to vacuum-tube cells. It didn't hurt the man and it didn't make the machine into a monster.

But they made Burckhardt uncomfortable all the same.

He put Barth and the factory and all his other little irritations out of his mind and tackled the tax returns. It took him until noon to verify the figures—which Barth could have done out of his memory and his private ledger in ten minutes, Burckhardt resentfully reminded himself.

He sealed them in an envelope and walked out to Miss Mitkin. "Since Mr. Barth isn't here, we'd better go to lunch in shifts," he said. "You can go first."

"Thanks." Miss Mitkin languidly took her bag out of the desk drawer and began to apply makeup.

Burckhardt offered her the envelope. "Drop this in the mail for me, will you? Uh—wait a minute. I wonder if I ought to phone Mr. Barth to make sure. Did his wife say whether he was able to take phone calls?"

"Didn't say." Miss Mitkin blotted her lips carefully with a Kleenex. "Wasn't his wife, anyway. It was his daughter who called and left the message."

"The kid?" Burckhardt frowned. "I thought she was away at school."

"She called, that's all I know."

Burckhardt went back to his own office and stared distastefully at the unopened mail on his desk. He didn't like nightmares; they spoiled his whole day. He should have stayed in bed, like Barth.

*

A funny thing happened on his way home. There was a disturbance at the corner where he usually caught his bus—someone was screaming something about a new kind of deep-freeze—so he walked an extra block. He saw the bus coming and started to trot. But behind him, someone was calling his name. He looked over his shoulder; a small harried-looking man was hurrying toward him.

Burckhardt hesitated, and then recognized him. It was a casual acquaintance named Swanson. Burckhardt sourly observed that he had already missed the bus.

He said, "Hello."

Swanson's face was desperately eager. "Burckhardt?" he asked inquiringly, with an odd intensity. And then he just stood there silently, watching Burckhardt's face, with a burning eagerness that dwindled to a faint hope and died to a regret. He was searching for something, waiting for something, Burckhardt thought. But whatever it was he wanted, Burckhardt didn't know how to supply it.

Burckhardt coughed and said again, "Hello, Swanson."

Swanson didn't even acknowledge the greeting. He merely sighed a very deep sigh.

"Nothing doing," he mumbled, apparently to himself. He nodded abstractedly to Burckhardt and turned away.

Burckhardt watched the slumped shoulders disappear in the crowd. It was an *odd* sort of day, he thought, and one he didn't much like. Things weren't going right.

Riding home on the next bus, he brooded about it. It wasn't anything terrible or disastrous; it was something out of his experience entirely. You live your life, like any man, and you form a network of impressions and reactions. You *expect* things. When you open your medicine chest, your razor is expected to be on the second shelf; when you lock your front door, you expect to have to give it a slight extra tug to make it latch.

It isn't the things that are right and perfect in your life that make it familiar. It is the things that are just a little bit wrong—the sticking latch, the light switch at the head of the stairs that needs an extra push because the spring is old and weak, the rug that unfailingly skids underfoot.

It wasn't just that things were wrong with the pattern of Burckhardt's life; it was that the *wrong* things were wrong. For instance, Barth hadn't come into the office, yet Barth *always* came in.

Burckhardt brooded about it through dinner. He brooded about it, despite his wife's attempt to interest him in a game of bridge with the neighbors, all through the evening. The neighbors were people he liked—Anne and Farley Dennerman. He had known them all their lives. But they were odd and brooding, too, this night and he barely listened to Dennerman's complaints about not being able to get good phone service or his wife's comments on the disgusting variety of television commercials they had these days.

Burckhardt was well on the way to setting an all-time record for continuous abstraction when, around midnight, with a suddenness that surprised him—he was strangely *aware* of it happening—he turned over in his bed and, quickly and completely, fell asleep.

II

On the morning of June 15th, Burckhardt woke up screaming.

It was more real than any dream he had ever had in his life. He could still hear the explosion, feel the blast that crushed him against a wall. It did not seem right that he should be sitting bolt upright in bed in an undisturbed room.

His wife came pattering up the stairs. "Darling!" she cried. "What's the matter?"

He mumbled, "Nothing. Bad dream."

She relaxed, hand on heart. In an angry tone, she started to say: "You gave me such a shock—"

But a noise from outside interrupted her. There was a wail of sirens and a clang of bells; it was loud and shocking.

The Burckhardts stared at each other for a heartbeat, then hurried fearfully to the window.

There were no rumbling fire engines in the street, only a small panel truck, cruising slowly along. Flaring loudspeaker horns crowned its top. From them issued the screaming sound of sirens, growing in intensity, mixed with the rumble of heavy-duty engines and the sound of bells. It was a perfect record of fire engines arriving at a four-alarm blaze.

Burckhardt said in amazement, "Mary, that's against the law! Do you know what they're doing? They're playing records of a fire. What are they up to?"

"Maybe it's a practical joke," his wife offered.

"Joke? Waking up the whole neighborhood at six o'clock in the morning?" He shook his head. "The police will be here in ten minutes," he predicted. "Wait and see."

But the police weren't—not in ten minutes, or at all. Whoever the pranksters in the car were, they apparently had a police permit for their games.

The car took a position in the middle of the block and stood silent for a few minutes. Then there was a crackle from the speaker, and a giant voice chanted:

"Feckle Freezers! Feckle Freezers! Gotta have a Feckle Freezer! Feckle, Feckle, Feckle, Feckle, Feckle, Feckle—"

It went on and on. Every house on the block had faces staring out of windows by then. The voice was not merely loud; it was nearly deafening.

Burckhardt shouted to his wife, over the uproar, "What the hell is a Feckle Freezer?"

"Some kind of a freezer, I guess, dear," she shrieked back unhelpfully.

*

Abruptly the noise stopped and the truck stood silent. It was still misty morning; the Sun's rays came horizontally across the rooftops. It was impossible to believe that, a moment ago, the silent block had been bellowing the name of a freezer.

"A crazy advertising trick," Burckhardt said bitterly. He yawned and turned away from the window. "Might as well get dressed. I guess that's the end of—"

The bellow caught him from behind; it was almost like a hard slap on the ears. A harsh, sneering voice, louder than the arch-angel's trumpet, howled:

"Have you got a freezer? *It stinks*! If it isn't a Feckle Freezer, *it stinks*! If it's a last year's Feckle Freezer, *it stinks*! Only this year's Feckle Freezer is any good at all! You know who owns an Ajax Freezer? Fairies own Ajax Freezers! You know who owns a Triplecold Freezer? Commies own Triplecold Freezers! Every freezer but a brand-new Feckle Freezer *stinks*!"

The voice screamed inarticulately with rage. "I'm warning you! Get out and buy a Feckle Freezer right away! Hurry up! Hurry for Feckle! Hurry for Feckle! Hurry, hurry, hurry, Feckle, Feckle, Feckle, Feckle, Feckle, Feckle...."

It stopped eventually. Burckhardt licked his lips. He started to say to his wife, "Maybe we ought to call the police about—" when the speakers erupted again. It caught him off guard; it was intended to catch him off guard. It screamed:

"Feckle, Feckle, Feckle, Feckle, Feckle, Feckle, Feckle, Feckle. Cheap freezers ruin your food. You'll get sick and throw up. You'll get sick and die. Buy a Feckle, Feckle, Feckle, Feckle! Ever take a piece of meat out of the freezer you've got and see how rotten and moldy it is? Buy a Feckle, Feckle, Feckle, Feckle, Feckle. Do you want to eat rotten, stinking food? Or do you want to wise up and buy a Feckle, Feckle, Feckle—"

That did it. With fingers that kept stabbing the wrong holes, Burckhardt finally managed to dial the local police station. He got a busy signal—it was apparent that he was not the only one with the same idea—and while he was shakingly dialing again, the noise outside stopped.

He looked out the window. The truck was gone.

*

Burckhardt loosened his tie and ordered another Frosty-Flip from the waiter. If only they wouldn't keep the Crystal Cafe so *hot*! The new paint job—searing reds and blinding yellows—was bad enough, but someone seemed to have the delusion that this was January instead of June; the place was a good ten degrees warmer than outside.

He swallowed the Frosty-Flip in two gulps. It had a kind of peculiar flavor, he thought, but not bad. It certainly cooled you off, just as the waiter had promised. He reminded himself to pick up a carton of them on the way home; Mary might like them. She was always interested in something new.

He stood up awkwardly as the girl came across the restaurant toward him. She was the most beautiful thing he had ever seen in Tylerton. Chin-height, honey-blonde hair and a figure that—well, it was all hers. There was no doubt in the world that the dress that clung to her was the only thing she wore. He felt as if he were blushing as she greeted him.

"Mr. Burckhardt." The voice was like distant tomtoms. "It's wonderful of you to let me see you, after this morning."

He cleared his throat. "Not at all. Won't you sit down, Miss—"

"April Horn," she murmured, sitting down—beside him, not where he had pointed on the other side of the table. "Call me April, won't you?"

She was wearing some kind of perfume, Burckhardt noted with what little of his mind was functioning at all. It didn't seem fair that she should be using perfume as well as everything else. He came to with a start and realized that the waiter was leaving with an order for *filets mignon* for two.

"Hey!" he objected.

"Please, Mr. Burckhardt." Her shoulder was against his, her face was turned to him, her breath was warm, her expression was tender and solicitous. "This is all on the Feckle Corporation. Please let them—it's the *least* they can do."

He felt her hand burrowing into his pocket.

"I put the price of the meal into your pocket," she whispered conspiratorially. "Please do that for me, won't you? I mean I'd appreciate it if you'd pay the waiter—I'm old-fashioned about things like that."

She smiled meltingly, then became mock-businesslike. "But you must take the money," she insisted. "Why, you're letting Feckle off lightly if you do! You could sue them for every nickel they've got, disturbing your sleep like that."

*

With a dizzy feeling, as though he had just seen someone make a rabbit disappear into a top hat, he said, "Why, it really wasn't so bad, uh, April. A little noisy, maybe, but—"

"Oh, Mr. Burckhardt!" The blue eyes were wide and admiring. "I knew you'd understand. It's just that—well, it's such a *wonderful* freezer that some of the outside men get carried away, so to speak. As soon as the main office found out about what happened, they sent representatives around to every house on the block to apologize. Your wife told us where we could phone you—and I'm so very pleased that you were willing to let me have lunch with you, so that I could apologize, too. Because truly, Mr. Burckhardt, it is a *fine* freezer.

"I shouldn't tell you this, but—" the blue eyes were shyly lowered—"I'd do almost anything for Feckle Freezers. It's more than a job to me." She looked up. She was enchanting. "I bet you think I'm silly, don't you?"

Burckhardt coughed. "Well, I—"

"Oh, you don't want to be unkind!" She shook her head. "No, don't pretend. You think it's silly. But really, Mr. Burckhardt, you wouldn't think so if you knew more about the Feckle. Let me show you this little booklet—"

Burckhardt got back from lunch a full hour late. It wasn't only the girl who delayed him. There had been a curious interview with a little man named Swanson, whom he barely knew, who had stopped him with desperate urgency on the street—and then left him cold.

But it didn't matter much. Mr. Barth, for the first time since Burckhardt had worked there, was out for the day—leaving Burckhardt stuck with the quarterly tax returns.

What did matter, though, was that somehow he had signed a purchase order for a twelve-cubic-foot Feckle Freezer, upright model, self-defrosting, list price $625, with a ten per cent "courtesy" discount—"Because of that *horrid* affair this morning, Mr. Burckhardt," she had said.

And he wasn't sure how he could explain it to his wife.

*

He needn't have worried. As he walked in the front door, his wife said almost immediately, "I wonder if we can't afford a new freezer, dear. There was a man here to apologize about that noise and—well, we got to talking and—"

She had signed a purchase order, too.

It had been the damnedest day, Burckhardt thought later, on his way up to bed. But the day wasn't done with him yet. At the head of the stairs, the weakened spring in the electric light switch refused to click at all. He snapped it back and forth angrily and, of course, succeeded in jarring the tumbler out of its pins. The wires shorted and every light in the house went out.

"Damn!" said Guy Burckhardt.

"Fuse?" His wife shrugged sleepily. "Let it go till the morning, dear."

Burckhardt shook his head. "You go back to bed. I'll be right along."

It wasn't so much that he cared about fixing the fuse, but he was too restless for sleep. He disconnected the bad switch with a screwdriver, stumbled down into the black kitchen, found the flashlight and climbed gingerly down the cellar stairs. He located a spare fuse, pushed an empty trunk over to the fuse box to stand on and twisted out the old fuse.

When the new one was in, he heard the starting click and steady drone of the refrigerator in the kitchen overhead.

He headed back to the steps, and stopped.

Where the old trunk had been, the cellar floor gleamed oddly bright. He inspected it in the flashlight beam. It was metal!

"Son of a gun," said Guy Burckhardt. He shook his head unbelievingly. He peered closer, rubbed the edges of the metallic patch with his thumb and acquired an annoying cut—the edges were *sharp*.

The stained cement floor of the cellar was a thin shell. He found a hammer and cracked it off in a dozen spots—everywhere was metal.

The whole cellar was a copper box. Even the cement-brick walls were false fronts over a metal sheath!

*

Baffled, he attacked one of the foundation beams. That, at least, was real wood. The glass in the cellar windows was real glass.

He sucked his bleeding thumb and tried the base of the cellar stairs. Real wood. He chipped at the bricks under the oil burner. Real bricks. The retaining walls, the floor—they were faked.

It was as though someone had shored up the house with a frame of metal and then laboriously concealed the evidence.

The biggest surprise was the upside-down boat hull that blocked the rear half of the cellar, relic of a brief home workshop period that

Burckhardt had gone through a couple of years before. From above, it looked perfectly normal. Inside, though, where there should have been thwarts and seats and lockers, there was a mere tangle of braces, rough and unfinished.

"But I *built* that!" Burckhardt exclaimed, forgetting his thumb. He leaned against the hull dizzily, trying to think this thing through. For reasons beyond his comprehension, someone had taken his boat and his cellar away, maybe his whole house, and replaced them with a clever mock-up of the real thing.

"That's crazy," he said to the empty cellar. He stared around in the light of the flash. He whispered, "What in the name of Heaven would anybody do that for?"

Reason refused an answer; there wasn't any reasonable answer. For long minutes, Burckhardt contemplated the uncertain picture of his own sanity.

He peered under the boat again, hoping to reassure himself that it was a mistake, just his imagination. But the sloppy, unfinished bracing was unchanged. He crawled under for a better look, feeling the rough wood incredulously. Utterly impossible!

He switched off the flashlight and started to wriggle out. But he didn't make it. In the moment between the command to his legs to move and the crawling out, he felt a sudden draining weariness flooding through him.

Consciousness went—not easily, but as though it were being taken away, and Guy Burckhardt was asleep.

III

On the morning of June 16th, Guy Burckhardt woke up in a cramped position huddled under the hull of the boat in his basement—and raced upstairs to find it was June 15th.

The first thing he had done was to make a frantic, hasty inspection of the boat hull, the faked cellar floor, the imitation stone. They were all as he had remembered them—all completely unbelievable.

The kitchen was its placid, unexciting self. The electric clock was purring soberly around the dial. Almost six o'clock, it said. His wife would be waking at any moment.

Burckhardt flung open the front door and stared out into the quiet street. The morning paper was tossed carelessly against the steps—and as he retrieved it, he noticed that this was the 15th day of June.

But that was impossible. *Yesterday* was the 15th of June. It was not a date one would forget—it was quarterly tax-return day.

He went back into the hall and picked up the telephone; he dialed for Weather Information, and got a well-modulated chant: "—and cooler, some showers. Barometric pressure thirty point zero four, rising ... United States Weather Bureau forecast for June 15th. Warm and sunny, with high around—"

He hung the phone up. June 15th.

"Holy heaven!" Burckhardt said prayerfully. Things were very odd indeed. He heard the ring of his wife's alarm and bounded up the stairs.

Mary Burckhardt was sitting upright in bed with the terrified, uncomprehending stare of someone just waking out of a nightmare.

"Oh!" she gasped, as her husband came in the room. "Darling, I just had the most *terrible* dream! It was like an explosion and—"

"Again?" Burckhardt asked, not very sympathetically. "Mary, something's funny! I *knew* there was something wrong all day yesterday and—"

He went on to tell her about the copper box that was the cellar, and the odd mock-up someone had made of his boat. Mary looked astonished, then alarmed, then placatory and uneasy.

She said, "Dear, are you *sure*? Because I was cleaning that old trunk out just last week and I didn't notice anything."

"Positive!" said Guy Burckhardt. "I dragged it over to the wall to step on it to put a new fuse in after we blew the lights out and—"

"After we what?" Mary was looking more than merely alarmed.

"After we blew the lights out. You know, when the switch at the head of the stairs stuck. I went down to the cellar and—"

Mary sat up in bed. "Guy, the switch didn't stick. I turned out the lights myself last night."

Burckhardt glared at his wife. "Now I *know* you didn't! Come here and take a look!"

He stalked out to the landing and dramatically pointed to the bad switch, the one that he had unscrewed and left hanging the night before....

Only it wasn't. It was as it had always been. Unbelieving, Burckhardt pressed it and the lights sprang up in both halls.

*

Mary, looking pale and worried, left him to go down to the kitchen and start breakfast. Burckhardt stood staring at the switch for a long time. His mental processes were gone beyond the point of disbelief and shock; they simply were not functioning.

He shaved and dressed and ate his breakfast in a state of numb introspection. Mary didn't disturb him; she was apprehensive and soothing. She kissed him good-by as he hurried out to the bus without another word.

Miss Mitkin, at the reception desk, greeted him with a yawn. "Morning," she said drowsily. "Mr. Barth won't be in today."

Burckhardt started to say something, but checked himself. She would not know that Barth hadn't been in yesterday, either, because she was tearing a June 14th pad off her calendar to make way for the "new" June 15th sheet.

He staggered to his own desk and stared unseeingly at the morning's mail. It had not even been opened yet, but he knew that the Factory Distributors envelope contained an order for twenty thousand feet of the new acoustic tile, and the one from Finebeck & Sons was a complaint.

After a long while, he forced himself to open them. They were.

By lunchtime, driven by a desperate sense of urgency, Burckhardt made Miss Mitkin take her lunch hour first—the June-fifteenth-that-was-yesterday, *he* had gone first. She went, looking vaguely worried about his strained insistence, but it made no difference to Burckhardt's mood.

The phone rang and Burckhardt picked it up abstractedly. "Contro Chemicals Downtown, Burckhardt speaking."

The voice said, "This is Swanson," and stopped.

Burckhardt waited expectantly, but that was all. He said, "Hello?"

Again the pause. Then Swanson asked in sad resignation, "Still nothing, eh?"

"Nothing what? Swanson, is there something you want? You came up to me yesterday and went through this routine. You—"

The voice crackled: "Burckhardt! Oh, my good heavens, *you remember*! Stay right there—I'll be down in half an hour!"

"What's this all about?"

"Never mind," the little man said exultantly. "Tell you about it when I see you. Don't say any more over the phone—somebody may be listening. Just wait there. Say, hold on a minute. Will you be alone in the office?"

"Well, no. Miss Mitkin will probably—"

"Hell. Look, Burckhardt, where do you eat lunch? Is it good and noisy?"

"Why, I suppose so. The Crystal Cafe. It's just about a block—"

"I know where it is. Meet you in half an hour!" And the receiver clicked.

*

The Crystal Cafe was no longer painted red, but the temperature was still up. And they had added piped-in music interspersed with commercials. The advertisements were for Frosty-Flip, Marlin Cigarettes—"They're sanitized," the announcer purred—and something called Choco-Bite candy bars that Burckhardt couldn't remember ever having heard of before. But he heard more about them quickly enough.

While he was waiting for Swanson to show up, a girl in the cellophane skirt of a nightclub cigarette vendor came through the restaurant with a tray of tiny scarlet-wrapped candies.

"Choco-Bites are *tangy*," she was murmuring as she came close to his table. "Choco-Bites are *tangier* than tangy!"

Burckhardt, intent on watching for the strange little man who had phoned him, paid little attention. But as she scattered a handful of the confections over the table next to his, smiling at the occupants, he caught a glimpse of her and turned to stare.

"Why, Miss Horn!" he said.

The girl dropped her tray of candies.

Burckhardt rose, concerned over the girl. "Is something wrong?"

But she fled.

The manager of the restaurant was staring suspiciously at Burckhardt, who sank back in his seat and tried to look inconspicuous. He hadn't insulted the girl! Maybe she was just a very strictly reared young lady, he thought—in spite of the long bare legs under the cellophane skirt—and when he addressed her, she thought he was a masher.

Ridiculous idea. Burckhardt scowled uneasily and picked up his menu.

"Burckhardt!" It was a shrill whisper.

Burckhardt looked up over the top of his menu, startled. In the seat across from him, the little man named Swanson was sitting, tensely poised.

"Burckhardt!" the little man whispered again. "Let's get out of here! They're on to you now. If you want to stay alive, come on!"

There was no arguing with the man. Burckhardt gave the hovering manager a sick, apologetic smile and followed Swanson out. The little man seemed to know where he was going. In the street, he clutched Burckhardt by the elbow and hurried him off down the block.

"Did you see her?" he demanded. "That Horn woman, in the phone booth? She'll have them here in five minutes, believe me, so hurry it up!"

*

Although the street was full of people and cars, nobody was paying any attention to Burckhardt and Swanson. The air had a nip in it—more like October than June, Burckhardt thought, in spite of the weather bureau. And he felt like a fool, following this mad little man down the street, running away from some "them" toward—toward what? The little man might be crazy, but he was afraid. And the fear was infectious.

"In here!" panted the little man.

It was another restaurant—more of a bar, really, and a sort of second-rate place that Burckhardt had never patronized.

"Right straight through," Swanson whispered; and Burckhardt, like a biddable boy, side-stepped through the mass of tables to the far end of the restaurant.

It was "L"-shaped, with a front on two streets at right angles to each other. They came out on the side street, Swanson staring coldly back at the question-looking cashier, and crossed to the opposite sidewalk.

They were under the marquee of a movie theater. Swanson's expression began to relax.

"Lost them!" he crowed softly. "We're almost there."

He stepped up to the window and bought two tickets. Burckhardt trailed him in to the theater. It was a weekday matinee and the place was almost empty. From the screen came sounds of gunfire and horse's hoofs. A solitary usher, leaning against a bright brass rail, looked briefly at them and went back to staring boredly at the picture as Swanson led Burckhardt down a flight of carpeted marble steps.

They were in the lounge and it was empty. There was a door for men and one for ladies; and there was a third door, marked "MANAGER" in gold letters. Swanson listened at the door, and gently opened it and peered inside.

"Okay," he said, gesturing.

Burckhardt followed him through an empty office, to another door—a closet, probably, because it was unmarked.

But it was no closet. Swanson opened it warily, looked inside, then motioned Burckhardt to follow.

It was a tunnel, metal-walled, brightly lit. Empty, it stretched vacantly away in both directions from them.

Burckhardt looked wondering around. One thing he knew and knew full well:

No such tunnel belonged under Tylerton.

*

There was a room off the tunnel with chairs and a desk and what looked like television screens. Swanson slumped in a chair, panting.

"We're all right for a while here," he wheezed. "They don't come here much any more. If they do, we'll hear them and we can hide."

"Who?" demanded Burckhardt.

The little man said, "Martians!" His voice cracked on the word and the life seemed to go out of him. In morose tones, he went on: "Well, I think they're Martians. Although you could be right, you know; I've had plenty of time to think it over these last few weeks, after they got you, and it's possible they're Russians after all. Still—"

"Start from the beginning. Who got me when?"

Swanson sighed. "So we have to go through the whole thing again. All right. It was about two months ago that you banged on my door, late at night. You were all beat up—scared silly. You begged me to help you—"

"I did?"

"Naturally you don't remember any of this. Listen and you'll understand. You were talking a blue streak about being captured and threatened, and your wife being dead and coming back to life, and all kinds of mixed-up nonsense. I thought you were crazy. But—well, I've always had a lot of respect for you. And you begged me to hide you and I have this darkroom, you know. It locks from the inside only. I put the lock on myself. So we went in there—just to humor you—and along about midnight, which was only fifteen or twenty minutes after, we passed out."

"Passed out?"

Swanson nodded. "Both of us. It was like being hit with a sandbag. Look, didn't that happen to you again last night?"

"I guess it did," Burckhardt shook his head uncertainly.

"Sure. And then all of a sudden we were awake again, and you said you were going to show me something funny, and we went out and bought a paper. And the date on it was June 15th."

"June 15th? But that's today! I mean—"

"You got it, friend. It's *always* today!"

It took time to penetrate.

Burckhardt said wonderingly, "You've hidden out in that darkroom for how many weeks?"

"How can I tell? Four or five, maybe. I lost count. And every day the same—always the 15th of June, always my landlady, Mrs. Keefer, is sweeping the front steps, always the same headline in the papers at the corner. It gets monotonous, friend."

IV

It was Burckhardt's idea and Swanson despised it, but he went along. He was the type who always went along.

"It's dangerous," he grumbled worriedly. "Suppose somebody comes by? They'll spot us and—"

"What have we got to lose?"

Swanson shrugged. "It's dangerous," he said again. But he went along.

Burckhardt's idea was very simple. He was sure of only one thing—the tunnel went somewhere. Martians or Russians, fantastic plot or crazy hallucination, whatever was wrong with Tylerton had an explanation, and the place to look for it was at the end of the tunnel.

They jogged along. It was more than a mile before they began to see an end. They were in luck—at least no one came through the tunnel to spot them. But Swanson had said that it was only at certain hours that the tunnel seemed to be in use.

Always the fifteenth of June. Why? Burckhardt asked himself. Never mind the how. *Why?*

And falling asleep, completely involuntarily—everyone at the same time, it seemed. And not remembering, never remembering anything—Swanson had said how eagerly he saw Burckhardt again, the morning after Burckhardt had incautiously waited five minutes too many before retreating into the darkroom. When Swanson had come to, Burckhardt was gone. Swanson had seen him in the street that afternoon, but Burckhardt had remembered nothing.

And Swanson had lived his mouse's existence for weeks, hiding in the woodwork at night, stealing out by day to search for Burckhardt in pitiful hope, scurrying around the fringe of life, trying to keep from the deadly eyes of *them.*

Them. One of "them" was the girl named April Horn. It was by seeing her walk carelessly into a telephone booth and never come out that Swanson had found the tunnel. Another was the man at the cigar stand in Burckhardt's office building. There were more, at least a dozen that Swanson knew of or suspected.

They were easy enough to spot, once you knew where to look—for they, alone in Tylerton, changed their roles from day to day. Burckhardt was on that 8:51 bus, every morning of every day-that-was-June-15th, never different by a hair or a moment. But April Horn was sometimes gaudy in the cellophane skirt, giving away candy or cigarettes; sometimes plainly dressed; sometimes not seen by Swanson at all.

Russians? Martians? Whatever they were, what could they be hoping to gain from this mad masquerade?

Burckhardt didn't know the answer—but perhaps it lay beyond the door at the end of the tunnel. They listened carefully and heard distant sounds that could not quite be made out, but nothing that seemed dangerous. They slipped through.

And, through a wide chamber and up a flight of steps, they found they were in what Burckhardt recognized as the Contro Chemicals plant.

*

Nobody was in sight. By itself, that was not so very odd—the automatized factory had never had very many persons in it. But Burckhardt remembered, from his single visit, the endless, ceaseless busyness of the plant, the valves that opened and closed, the vats that emptied themselves and filled themselves and stirred and cooked and chemically tasted the bubbling liquids they held inside themselves. The plant was never populated, but it was never still.

Only—now it *was* still. Except for the distant sounds, there was no breath of life in it. The captive electronic minds were sending out no commands; the coils and relays were at rest.

Burckhardt said, "Come on." Swanson reluctantly followed him through the tangled aisles of stainless steel columns and tanks.

They walked as though they were in the presence of the dead. In a way, they were, for what were the automatons that once had run the factory, if not corpses? The machines were controlled by computers that were really not computers at all, but the electronic analogues of living brains. And if they were turned off, were they not dead? For each had once been a human mind.

Take a master petroleum chemist, infinitely skilled in the separation of crude oil into its fractions. Strap him down, probe into his brain with searching electronic needles. The machine scans the patterns of the mind, translates what it sees into charts and sine waves. Impress these same waves on a robot computer and you have your chemist. Or a thousand copies of your chemist, if you wish, with all of his knowledge and skill, and no human limitations at all.

Put a dozen copies of him into a plant and they will run it all, twenty-four hours a day, seven days of every week, never tiring, never overlooking anything, never forgetting....

Swanson stepped up closer to Burckhardt. "I'm scared," he said.

They were across the room now and the sounds were louder. They were not machine sounds, but voices; Burckhardt moved cautiously up to a door and dared to peer around it.

It was a smaller room, lined with television screens, each one—a dozen or more, at least—with a man or woman sitting before it, staring into the screen and dictating notes into a recorder. The viewers dialed from scene to scene; no two screens ever showed the same picture.

The pictures seemed to have little in common. One was a store, where a girl dressed like April Horn was demonstrating home freezers. One was a series of shots of kitchens. Burckhardt caught a glimpse of what looked like the cigar stand in his office building.

It was baffling and Burckhardt would have loved to stand there and puzzle it out, but it was too busy a place. There was the chance that someone would look their way or walk out and find them.

*

They found another room. This one was empty. It was an office, large and sumptuous. It had a desk, littered with papers. Burckhardt stared at them, briefly at first—then, as the words on one of them caught his attention, with incredulous fascination.

He snatched up the topmost sheet, scanned it, and another, while Swanson was frenziedly searching through the drawers.

Burckhardt swore unbelievingly and dropped the papers to the desk.

Swanson, hardly noticing, yelped with delight: "Look!" He dragged a gun from the desk. "And it's loaded, too!"

Burckhardt stared at him blankly, trying to assimilate what he had read. Then, as he realized what Swanson had said, Burckhardt's eyes sparked. "Good man!" he cried. "We'll take it. We're getting out of here with that gun, Swanson. And we're going to the police! Not the cops in Tylerton, but the F.B.I., maybe. Take a look at this!"

The sheaf he handed Swanson was headed: "Test Area Progress Report. Subject: Marlin Cigarettes Campaign." It was mostly tabulated figures that made little sense to Burckhardt and Swanson, but at the end was a summary that said:

Although Test 47-K3 pulled nearly double the number of new users of any of the other tests conducted, it probably cannot be used in the field because of local sound-truck control ordinances.

The tests in the 47-K12 group were second best and our recommendation is that retests be conducted in this appeal, testing each of the three best campaigns with and without the addition of sampling techniques.

An alternative suggestion might be to proceed directly with the top appeal in the K12 series, if the client is unwilling to go to the expense of additional tests.

All of these forecast expectations have an 80% probability of being within one-half of one per cent of results forecast, and more than 99% probability of coming within 5%.

Swanson looked up from the paper into Burckhardt's eyes. "I don't get it," he complained.

Burckhardt said, "I don't blame you. It's crazy, but it fits the facts, Swanson, *it fits the facts*. They aren't Russians and they aren't Martians. These people are advertising men! Somehow—heaven knows how they did it—they've taken Tylerton over. They've got us, all of us, you and me and twenty or thirty thousand other people, right under their thumbs.

"Maybe they hypnotize us and maybe it's something else; but however they do it, what happens is that they let us live a day at a time. They pour advertising into us the whole damned day long. And at the end of the day, they see what happened—and then they wash the day out of our minds and start again the next day with different advertising."

*

Swanson's jaw was hanging. He managed to close it and swallow. "Nuts!" he said flatly.

Burckhardt shook his head. "Sure, it sounds crazy—but this whole thing is crazy. How else would you explain it? You can't deny that most of Tylerton lives the same day over and over again. You've *seen* it! And that's the crazy part and we have to admit that that's true—unless we are the crazy ones. And once you admit that somebody, somehow, knows how to accomplish that, the rest of it makes all kinds of sense.

"Think of it, Swanson! They test every last detail before they spend a nickel on advertising! Do you have any idea what that means? Lord knows how much money is involved, but I know for a fact that some companies spend twenty or thirty million dollars a year on advertising. Multiply it, say, by a hundred companies. Say that every one of them learns how to cut its advertising cost by only ten per cent. And that's peanuts, believe me!

"If they know in advance what's going to work, they can cut their costs in half—maybe to less than half, I don't know. But that's saving two or three hundred million dollars a year—and if they pay only ten or twenty per cent of that for the use of Tylerton, it's still dirt cheap for them and a fortune for whoever took over Tylerton."

Swanson licked his lips. "You mean," he offered hesitantly, "that we're a—well, a kind of captive audience?"

Burckhardt frowned. "Not exactly." He thought for a minute. "You know how a doctor tests something like penicillin? He sets up a series of little colonies of germs on gelatine disks and he tries the stuff on one after another, changing it a little each time. Well, that's us—we're the germs, Swanson. Only it's even more efficient than that. They don't have to test more than one colony, because they can use it over and over again."

It was too hard for Swanson to take in. He only said: "What do we do about it?"

"We go to the police. They can't use human beings for guinea pigs!"

"How do we get to the police?"

Burckhardt hesitated. "I think—" he began slowly. "Sure. This place is the office of somebody important. We've got a gun. We'll stay right here until he comes along. And he'll get us out of here."

Simple and direct. Swanson subsided and found a place to sit, against the wall, out of sight of the door. Burckhardt took up a position behind the door itself—

And waited.

*

The wait was not as long as it might have been. Half an hour, perhaps. Then Burckhardt heard approaching voices and had time for a swift whisper to Swanson before he flattened himself against the wall.

It was a man's voice, and a girl's. The man was saying, "—reason why you couldn't report on the phone? You're ruining your whole day's test! What the devil's the matter with you, Janet?"

"I'm sorry, Mr. Dorchin," she said in a sweet, clear tone. "I thought it was important."

The man grumbled, "Important! One lousy unit out of twenty-one thousand."

"But it's the Burckhardt one, Mr. Dorchin. Again. And the way he got out of sight, he must have had some help."

"All right, all right. It doesn't matter, Janet; the Choco-Bite program is ahead of schedule anyhow. As long as you're this far, come on in the office and make out your worksheet. And don't worry about the Burckhardt business. He's probably just wandering around. We'll pick him up tonight and—"

They were inside the door. Burckhardt kicked it shut and pointed the gun.

"That's what you think," he said triumphantly.

It was worth the terrified hours, the bewildered sense of insanity, the confusion and fear. It was the most satisfying sensation Burckhardt had ever had in his life. The expression on the man's face was one he had read about but never actually seen: Dorchin's mouth fell open and his eyes went wide, and though he managed to make a sound that might have been a question, it was not in words.

The girl was almost as surprised. And Burckhardt, looking at her, knew why her voice had been so familiar. The girl was the one who had introduced herself to him as April Horn.

Dorchin recovered himself quickly. "Is this the one?" he asked sharply.

The girl said, "Yes."

Dorchin nodded. "I take it back. You were right. Uh, you—Burckhardt. What do you want?"

*

Swanson piped up, "Watch him! He might have another gun."

"Search him then," Burckhardt said. "I'll tell you what we want, Dorchin. We want you to come along with us to the FBI and explain to them how you can get away with kidnapping twenty thousand people."

"Kidnapping?" Dorchin snorted. "That's ridiculous, man! Put that gun away—you can't get away with this!"

Burckhardt hefted the gun grimly. "I think I can."

Dorchin looked furious and sick—but, oddly, not afraid. "Damn it—" he started to bellow, then closed his mouth and swallowed. "Listen," he said persuasively, "you're making a big mistake. I haven't kidnapped anybody, believe me!"

"I don't believe you," said Burckhardt bluntly. "Why should I?"

"But it's true! Take my word for it!"

Burckhardt shook his head. "The FBI can take your word if they like. We'll find out. Now how do we get out of here?"

Dorchin opened his mouth to argue.

Burckhardt blazed: "Don't get in my way! I'm willing to kill you if I have to. Don't you understand that? I've gone through two days of hell and every second of it I blame on you. Kill you? It would be a pleasure and I don't have a thing in the world to lose! Get us out of here!"

Dorchin's face went suddenly opaque. He seemed about to move; but the blonde girl he had called Janet slipped between him and the gun.

"Please!" she begged Burckhardt. "You don't understand. You mustn't shoot!"

"*Get out of my way!*"

"But, Mr. Burckhardt—"

She never finished. Dorchin, his face unreadable, headed for the door. Burckhardt had been pushed one degree too far. He swung the gun, bellowing. The girl called out sharply. He pulled the trigger. Closing on him with pity and pleading in her eyes, she came again between the gun and the man.

Burckhardt aimed low instinctively, to cripple, not to kill. But his aim was not good.

The pistol bullet caught her in the pit of the stomach.

*

Dorchin was out and away, the door slamming behind him, his footsteps racing into the distance.

Burckhardt hurled the gun across the room and jumped to the girl.

Swanson was moaning. "That finishes us, Burckhardt. Oh, why did you do it? We could have got away. We could have gone to the police. We were practically out of here! We—"

Burckhardt wasn't listening. He was kneeling beside the girl. She lay flat on her back, arms helter-skelter. There was no blood, hardly any sign of the wound; but the position in which she lay was one that no living human being could have held.

Yet she wasn't dead.

She wasn't dead—and Burckhardt, frozen beside her, thought: *She isn't alive, either.*

There was no pulse, but there was a rhythmic ticking of the outstretched fingers of one hand.

There was no sound of breathing, but there was a hissing, sizzling noise.

The eyes were open and they were looking at Burckhardt. There was neither fear nor pain in them, only a pity deeper than the Pit.

She said, through lips that writhed erratically, "Don't—worry, Mr. Burckhardt. I'm—all right."

Burckhardt rocked back on his haunches, staring. Where there should have been blood, there was a clean break of a substance that was not flesh; and a curl of thin golden-copper wire.

Burckhardt moistened his lips.

"You're a robot," he said.

The girl tried to nod. The twitching lips said, "I am. And so are you."

V

Swanson, after a single inarticulate sound, walked over to the desk and sat staring at the wall. Burckhardt rocked back and forth beside the shattered puppet on the floor. He had no words.

The girl managed to say, "I'm—sorry all this happened." The lovely lips twisted into a rictus sneer, frightening on that smooth young face, until she got them under control. "Sorry," she said again. "The—nerve center was right about where the bullet hit. Makes it difficult to—control this body."

Burckhardt nodded automatically, accepting the apology. Robots. It was obvious, now that he knew it. In hindsight, it was inevitable. He thought of his mystic notions of hypnosis or Martians or something stranger still—idiotic, for the simple fact of created robots fitted the facts better and more economically.

All the evidence had been before him. The automatized factory, with its transplanted minds—why not transplant a mind into a humanoid robot, give it its original owner's features and form?

Could it know that it was a robot?

"All of us," Burckhardt said, hardly aware that he spoke out loud. "My wife and my secretary and you and the neighbors. All of us the same."

"No." The voice was stronger. "Not exactly the same, all of us. I chose it, you see. I—" this time the convulsed lips were not a random contortion of the nerves—" I was an ugly woman, Mr. Burckhardt, and nearly sixty years old. Life had passed me. And when Mr. Dorchin offered me the chance to live again as a beautiful girl, I jumped at the opportunity. Believe me, I *jumped*, in spite of its disadvantages. My flesh body is still alive—it is sleeping, while I am here. I could go back to it. But I never do."

"And the rest of us?"

"Different, Mr. Burckhardt. I work here. I'm carrying out Mr. Dorchin's orders, mapping the results of the advertising tests, watching you and the others live as he makes you live. I do it by choice, but you have no choice. Because, you see, you are dead."

"Dead?" cried Burckhardt; it was almost a scream.

The blue eyes looked at him unwinkingly and he knew that it was no lie. He swallowed, marveling at the intricate mechanisms that let him swallow, and sweat, and eat.

He said: "Oh. The explosion in my dream."

"It was no dream. You are right—the explosion. That was real and this plant was the cause of it. The storage tanks let go and what the blast didn't get, the fumes killed a little later. But almost everyone died in the blast, twenty-one thousand persons. You died with them and that was Dorchin's chance."

"The damned ghoul!" said Burckhardt.

*

The twisted shoulders shrugged with an odd grace. "Why? You were gone. And you and all the others were what Dorchin wanted—a whole town, a perfect slice of America. It's as easy to transfer a pattern from a dead brain as a living one. Easier—the dead can't say no. Oh, it took work and money—the town was a wreck—but it was possible to rebuild it entirely, especially because it wasn't necessary to have all the details exact.

"There were the homes where even the brains had been utterly destroyed, and those are empty inside, and the cellars that needn't be too perfect, and the streets that hardly matter. And anyway, it only has to last for one day. The same day—June 15th—over and over again; and if someone finds something a little wrong, somehow, the discovery won't have time to snowball, wreck the validity of the tests, because all errors are canceled out at midnight."

The face tried to smile. "That's the dream, Mr. Burckhardt, that day of June 15th, because you never really lived it. It's a present from Mr. Dorchin, a dream that he gives you and then takes back at the end of the day, when he has all his figures on how many of you responded to what variation of which appeal, and the maintenance crews go down the tunnel to go through the whole city, washing out the new dream with their little electronic drains, and then the dream starts all over again. On June 15th.

"Always June 15th, because June 14th is the last day any of you can remember alive. Sometimes the crews miss someone—as they missed you, because you were under your boat. But it doesn't matter. The ones who are missed give themselves away if they show it—and if they don't, it doesn't affect the test. But they don't drain us, the ones of us who work for Dorchin. We sleep when the power is turned off, just as you do. When we wake up, though, we remember." The face contorted wildly. "If I could only forget!"

Burckhardt said unbelievingly, "All this to sell merchandise! It must have cost millions!"

The robot called April Horn said, "It did. But it has made millions for Dorchin, too. And that's not the end of it. Once he finds the master words that make people act, do you suppose he will stop with that? Do you suppose—"

The door opened, interrupting her. Burckhardt whirled. Belatedly remembering Dorchin's flight, he raised the gun.

"Don't shoot," ordered the voice calmly. It was not Dorchin; it was another robot, this one not disguised with the clever plastics and cosmetics, but shining plain. It said metallically: "Forget it, Burckhardt. You're not accomplishing anything. Give me that gun before you do any more damage. Give it to me *now*."

*

Burckhardt bellowed angrily. The gleam on this robot torso was steel; Burckhardt was not at all sure that his bullets would pierce it, or do much harm if they did. He would have put it to the test—

But from behind him came a whimpering, scurrying whirlwind; its name was Swanson, hysterical with fear. He catapulted into Burckhardt and sent him sprawling, the gun flying free.

"Please!" begged Swanson incoherently, prostrate before the steel robot. "He would have shot you—please don't hurt me! Let me work for you, like that girl. I'll do anything, anything you tell me—"

The robot voice said. "We don't need your help." It took two precise steps and stood over the gun—and spurned it, left it lying on the floor.

The wrecked blonde robot said, without emotion, "I doubt that I can hold out much longer, Mr. Dorchin."

"Disconnect if you have to," replied the steel robot.

Burckhardt blinked. "But you're not Dorchin!"

The steel robot turned deep eyes on him. "I am," it said. "Not in the flesh—but this is the body I am using at the moment. I doubt that you can damage this one with the gun. The other robot body was more vulnerable. Now will you stop this nonsense? I don't want to have to damage you; you're too expensive for that. Will you just sit down and let the maintenance crews adjust you?"

Swanson groveled. "You—you won't punish us?"

The steel robot had no expression, but its voice was almost surprised. "Punish you?" it repeated on a rising note. "How?"

Swanson quivered as though the word had been a whip; but Burckhardt flared: "Adjust *him*, if he'll let you—but not me! You're going to have to do me a lot of damage, Dorchin. I don't care what I cost or how much trouble it's going to be to put me back together again. But I'm going out of that door! If you want to stop me, you'll have to kill me. You won't stop me any other way!"

The steel robot took a half-step toward him, and Burckhardt involuntarily checked his stride. He stood poised and shaking, ready for death, ready for attack, ready for anything that might happen.

Ready for anything except what did happen. For Dorchin's steel body merely stepped aside, between Burckhardt and the gun, but leaving the door free.

"Go ahead," invited the steel robot. "Nobody's stopping you."

*

Outside the door, Burckhardt brought up sharp. It was insane of Dorchin to let him go! Robot or flesh, victim or beneficiary, there was nothing to stop him from going to the FBI or whatever law he could find away from Dorchin's synthetic empire, and telling his story. Surely the corporations who paid Dorchin for test results had no notion of the ghoul's technique he used; Dorchin would have to keep it from them, for the breath of publicity would put a stop to it. Walking out meant death, perhaps—but at that moment in his pseudo-life, death was no terror for Burckhardt.

There was no one in the corridor. He found a window and stared out of it. There was Tylerton—an ersatz city, but looking so real and familiar that Burckhardt almost imagined the whole episode a dream. It was no dream, though. He was certain of that in his heart and equally certain that nothing in Tylerton could help him now.

It had to be the other direction.

It took him a quarter of an hour to find a way, but he found it—skulking through the corridors, dodging the suspicion of footsteps, knowing for certain that his hiding was in vain, for Dorchin was undoubtedly aware of every move he made. But no one stopped him, and he found another door.

It was a simple enough door from the inside. But when he opened it and stepped out, it was like nothing he had ever seen.

First there was light—brilliant, incredible, blinding light. Burckhardt blinked upward, unbelieving and afraid.

He was standing on a ledge of smooth, finished metal. Not a dozen yards from his feet, the ledge dropped sharply away; he hardly dared approach the brink, but even from where he stood he could see no bottom to the chasm before him. And the gulf extended out of sight into the glare on either side of him.

*

No wonder Dorchin could so easily give him his freedom! From the factory, there was nowhere to go—but how incredible this fantastic gulf, how impossible the hundred white and blinding suns that hung above!

A voice by his side said inquiringly, "Burckhardt?" And thunder rolled the name, mutteringly soft, back and forth in the abyss before him.

Burckhardt wet his lips. "Y-yes?" he croaked.

"This is Dorchin. Not a robot this time, but Dorchin in the flesh, talking to you on a hand mike. Now you have seen, Burckhardt. Now will you be reasonable and let the maintenance crews take over?"

Burckhardt stood paralyzed. One of the moving mountains in the blinding glare came toward him.

It towered hundreds of feet over his head; he stared up at its top, squinting helplessly into the light.

It looked like—

Impossible!

The voice in the loudspeaker at the door said, "Burckhardt?" But he was unable to answer.

A heavy rumbling sigh. "I see," said the voice. "You finally understand. There's no place to go. You know it now. I could have told you, but you might not have believed me, so it was better for you to see it yourself. And after all, Burckhardt, why would I reconstruct a city just the way it was before? I'm a businessman; I count costs. If a thing has to be full-scale, I build it that way. But there wasn't any need to in this case."

From the mountain before him, Burckhardt helplessly saw a lesser cliff descend carefully toward him. It was long and dark, and at the end of it was whiteness, five-fingered whiteness....

"Poor little Burckhardt," crooned the loudspeaker, while the echoes rumbled through the enormous chasm that was only a workshop. "It must have been quite a shock for you to find out you were living in a town built on a table top."

VI

It was the morning of June 15th, and Guy Burckhardt woke up screaming out of a dream.

It had been a monstrous and incomprehensible dream, of explosions and shadowy figures that were not men and terror beyond words.

He shuddered and opened his eyes.

Outside his bedroom window, a hugely amplified voice was howling.

Burckhardt stumbled over to the window and stared outside. There was an out-of-season chill to the air, more like October than June; but the scent was normal enough—except for the sound-truck that squatted at curbside halfway down the block. Its speaker horns blared:

"Are you a coward? Are you a fool? Are you going to let crooked politicians steal the country from you? NO! Are you going to put up with four more years of graft and crime? NO! Are you going to vote straight Federal Party all up and down the ballot? YES! *You just bet you are!*"

Sometimes he screams, sometimes he wheedles, threatens, begs, cajoles ... but his voice goes on and on through one June 15th after another.

THE HATED

The bar didn't have a name. No name of any kind. Not even an indication that it had ever had one. All it said on the outside was:

Cafe EAT *Cocktails*

which doesn't make a lot of sense. But it was a bar. It had a big TV set going ya-ta-ta ya-ta-ta in three glorious colors, and a jukebox that tried to drown out the TV with that lousy music they play. Anyway, it wasn't a kid hangout. I kind of like it. But I wasn't supposed to be there at all; it's in the contract. I was supposed to stay in New York and the New England states.

Cafe-EAT-*Cocktails* was right across the river. I think the name of the place was Hoboken, but I'm not sure. It all had a kind of dreamy feeling to it. I was—

Well, I couldn't even remember going there. I remembered one minute I was downtown New York, looking across the river. I did that a lot. And then I was there. I don't remember crossing the river at all.

I was drunk, you know.

*

You know how it is? Double bourbons and keep them coming. And after a while the bartender stops bringing me the ginger ale because gradually I forget to mix them. I got pretty loaded long before I left New York. I realize that. I guess I had to get pretty loaded to risk the pension and all.

Used to be I didn't drink much, but now, I don't know, when I have one drink, I get to thinking about Sam and Wally and Chowderhead and Gilvey and the captain. If I don't drink, I think about them, too, and then I take a drink. And that leads to another drink, and it all comes out to the same thing. Well, I guess I said it already, I drink a pretty good amount, but you can't blame me.

There was a girl.

I always get a girl someplace. Usually they aren't much and this one wasn't either. I mean she was probably somebody's mother. She was around thirty-five and not so bad, though she had a long scar under her ear down along her throat to the little round spot where her larynx was. It wasn't ugly. She smelled nice—while I could still smell, you know—and she didn't talk much. I liked that. Only—

Well, did you ever meet somebody with a nervous cough? Like when you say something funny—a little funny, not a big yock—they don't laugh and they don't stop with just smiling, but they sort of cough? She did that. I began to itch. I couldn't help it. I asked her to stop it.

She spilled her drink and looked at me almost as though she was scared—and I had tried to say it quietly, too.

"Sorry," she said, a little angry, a little scared. "*Sorry.* But you don't have to—"

"Forget it."

"Sure. But you asked me to sit down here with you, remember? If you're going to—"

"*Forget it!*" I nodded at the bartender and held up two fingers. "You need another drink," I said. "The thing is," I said, "Gilvey used to do that."

"What?"

"That cough."

She looked puzzled. "You mean like this?"

"*Goddam it, stop it!*" Even the bartender looked over at me that time. Now she was really mad, but I didn't want her to go away. I said, "Gilvey was a fellow who went to Mars with me. Pat Gilvey."

"*Oh.*" She sat down again and leaned across the table, low. "*Mars.*"

*

The bartender brought our drinks and looked at me suspiciously. I said, "Say, Mac, would you turn down the air-conditioning?"

"My name isn't Mac. No."

"Have a heart. It's too cold in here."

"Sorry." He didn't sound sorry.

I was cold. I mean that kind of weather, it's always cold in those places. You know around New York in August? It hits eighty,

eighty-five, ninety. All the places have air-conditioning and what they really want is for you to wear a shirt and tie.

But I like to walk a lot. You would, too, you know. And you can't walk around much in long pants and a suit coat and all that stuff. Not around there. Not in August. And so then, when I went into a bar, it'd have one of those built-in freezers for the used-car salesmen with their dates, or maybe their wives, all dressed up. For what? But I froze.

"*Mars*," the girl breathed. "*Mars*."

I began to itch again. "Want to dance?"

"They don't have a license," she said. "Byron, *I* didn't know you'd been to *Mars*! Please *tell* me about it."

"It was all right," I said.

That was a lie.

She was interested. She forgot to smile. It made her look nicer. She said, "I knew a man—my brother-in-law—he was my husband's brother—I mean my ex-husband—"

"I get the idea."

"He worked for General Atomic. In Rockford, Illinois. You know where that is?"

"Sure." I couldn't go there, but I knew where Illinois was.

"He worked on the first Mars ship. Oh, fifteen years ago, wasn't it? He always wanted to go himself, but he couldn't pass the tests." She stopped and looked at me.

I knew what she was thinking. But I didn't always look this way, you know. Not that there's anything wrong with me now, I mean, but I couldn't pass the tests any more. Nobody can. That's why we're all one-trippers.

I said, "The only reason I'm shaking like this is because I'm cold."

It wasn't true, of course. It was that cough of Gilvey's. I didn't like to think about Gilvey, or Sam or Chowderhead or Wally or the captain. I didn't like to think about any of them. It made me shake.

You see, we couldn't kill each other. They wouldn't let us do that. Before we took off, they did something to our minds to make sure.

What they did, it doesn't last forever. It lasts for two years and then it wears off. That's long enough, you see, because that gets you to Mars and back; and it's plenty long enough, in another way, because it's like a strait-jacket.

You know how to make a baby cry? Hold his hands. It's the most basic thing there is. What they did to us so we couldn't kill each other, it was like being tied up, like having our hands held so we couldn't get free. Well. But two years was long enough. Too long.

The bartender came over and said, "Pal, I'm sorry. See, I turned the air-conditioning down. You all right? You look so—"

I said, "Sure, I'm all right."

He sounded worried. I hadn't even heard him come back. The girl was looking worried, too, I guess because I was shaking so hard I was spilling my drink. I put some money on the table without even counting it.

"It's all right," I said. "We were just going."

"We were?" She looked confused. But she came along with me. They always do, once they find out you've been to Mars.

*

In the next place, she said, between trips to the powder room, "It must take a lot of courage to sign up for something like that. Were you scientifically inclined in school? Don't you have to know an awful lot to be a space-flyer? Did you ever see any of those little monkey characters they say live on Mars? I read an article about how they lived in little cities of pup-tents or something like that—only they didn't make them, they grew them. Funny! Ever see those? That trip must have been a real drag, I bet. What is it, nine months? You couldn't have a baby! Excuse me— Say, tell me. All that time, how'd you—well, manage things? I mean didn't you ever have to go to the you-know or anything?"

"We managed," I said.

She giggled, and that reminded her, so she went to the powder room again. I thought about getting up and leaving while she was gone, but what was the use of that? I'd only pick up somebody else.

It was nearly midnight. A couple of minutes wouldn't hurt. I reached in my pocket for the little box of pills they give us—it isn't refillable, but we get a new prescription in the mail every month, along with the pension check. The label on the box said:

CAUTION

Use only as directed by physician. Not to be taken by persons suffering heart condition, digestive upset or circulatory disease. Not to be used in conjunction with alcoholic beverages.

I took three of them. I don't like to start them before midnight, but anyway I stopped shaking.

I closed my eyes, and then I was on the ship again. The noise in the bar became the noise of the rockets and the air washers and the sludge sluicers. I began to sweat, although this place was air-conditioned, too.

I could hear Wally whistling to himself the way he did, the sound muffled by his oxygen mask and drowned in the rocket noise, but still perfectly audible. The tune was *Sophisticated Lady*. Sometimes it was *Easy to Love* and sometimes *Chasing Shadows*, but mostly *Sophisticated Lady*. He was from Juilliard.

Somebody sneezed, and it sounded just like Chowderhead sneezing. You know how everybody sneezes according to his own individual style? Chowderhead had a ladylike little sneeze; it went *hutta*, real quick, all through the mouth, no nose involved. The captain went *Hrasssh*; Wally was Ashoo, ashoo, *ashoo*. Gilvey was *Hutch*-uh. Sam didn't sneeze much, but he sort of coughed and sprayed, and that was worse.

Sometimes I used to think about killing Sam by tying him down and having Wally and the captain sneeze him to death. But that was a kind of a joke, naturally, when I was feeling good. Or pretty good. Usually I thought about a knife for Sam. For Chowderhead it was a gun, right in the belly, one shot. For Wally it was a tommy gun—just stitching him up and down, you know, back and forth. The captain I would put in a cage with hungry lions, and Gilvey I'd strangle with my bare hands. That was probably because of the cough, I guess.

*

She was back. "Please tell me about it," she begged. "I'm *so* curious."

I opened my eyes. "You want me to tell you about it?"

"Oh, please!"

"About what it's like to fly to Mars on a rocket?"

"Yes!"

"All right," I said.

It's wonderful what three little white pills will do. I wasn't even shaking.

"There's six men, see? In a space the size of a Buick, and that's all the room there is. Two of us in the bunks all the time, four of us on watch. Maybe you want to stay in the sack an extra ten minutes—because it's the only place on the ship where you can stretch out, you know, the only place where you can rest without somebody's elbow in your side. But you can't. Because by then it's the next man's turn.

"And maybe you don't have elbows in your side while it's your turn off watch, but in the starboard bunk there's the air-regenerator master valve—I bet I could still show you the bruises right around my kidneys—and in the port bunk there's the emergency-escape-hatch handle. That gets you right in the temple, if you turn your head too fast.

"And you can't really sleep, I mean not soundly, because of the noise. That is, when the rockets are going. When they aren't going, then you're in free-fall, and that's bad, too, because you dream about falling. But when they're going, I don't know, I think it's worse. It's pretty loud.

"And even if it weren't for the noise, if you sleep too soundly you might roll over on your oxygen line. Then you dream about drowning. Ever do that? You're strangling and choking and you can't get any air? It isn't dangerous, I guess. Anyway, it always woke me up in time. Though I heard about a fellow in a flight six years ago—

"Well. So you've always got this oxygen mask on, all the time, except if you take it off for a second to talk to somebody. You don't do that very often, because what is there to say? Oh, maybe the first couple of weeks, sure—everybody's friends then. You don't even need the mask, for that matter. Or not very much. Everybody's still pretty clean. The place smells—oh, let's see—about like the locker room in a gym. You know? You can stand it. That's if nobody's got space sickness, of course. We were lucky that way.

"But that's about how it's going to get anyway, you know. Outside the masks, it's soup. It isn't that you smell it so much. You kind of *taste* it, in the back of your mouth, and your eyes sting. That's after the first two or three months. Later on, it gets worse.

"And with the mask on, of course, the oxygen mixture is coming in under pressure. That's funny if you're not used to it. Your lungs have to work a little bit harder to get rid of it, especially when you're asleep, so after a while the muscles get sore. And then they get sorer. And then—

"Well.

"Before we take off, the psych people give us a long doo-da that keeps us from killing each other. But they can't stop us from thinking about it. And afterward, after we're back on Earth—this is what you won't read about in the articles—they keep us apart. You know how they work it? We get a pension, naturally. I mean there's got to be a pension, otherwise there isn't enough money in the world to make anybody go. But in the contract, it says to get the pension we have to stay in our own area.

"The whole country's marked off. Six sections. Each has at least one big city in it. I was lucky, I got a lot of them. They try to keep it so every man's home town is in his own section, but—well, like with us, Chowderhead and the captain both happened to come from Santa Monica. I think it was Chowderhead that got California, Nevada, all that Southwest area. It was the luck of the draw. God knows what the captain got.

"Maybe New Jersey," I said, and took another white pill.

*

We went on to another place and she said suddenly, "I figured something out. The way you keep looking around."

"What did you figure out?"

"Well, part of it was what you said about the other fellow getting New Jersey. This is New Jersey. You don't belong in this section, right?"

"Right," I said after a minute.

"So why are you here? I know why. You're here because you're looking for somebody."

"That's right."

She said triumphantly, "You want to find that other fellow from your crew! You want to fight him!"

I couldn't help shaking, white pills or no white pills. But I had to correct her.

"No. I want to kill him."

"How do you know he's here? He's got a lot of states to roam around in, too, doesn't he?"

"Six. New Jersey, Pennsylvania, Delaware, Maryland—all the way down to Washington."

"Then how do you know—"

"He'll be here." I didn't have to tell her how I knew. But I knew.

I wasn't the only one who spent his time at the border of his assigned area, looking across the river or staring across a state line, knowing that somebody was on the other side. I knew. You fight a war and you don't have to guess that the enemy might have his troops a thousand miles away from the battle line. You know where his troops will be. You know he wants to fight, too.

Hutta. Hutta.

I spilled my drink.

I looked at her. "You—you didn't—"

She looked frightened. "What's the matter?"

"*Did you just sneeze?*"

"Sneeze? Me? Did I—"

I said something quick and nasty, I don't know what. No! It hadn't been her. I knew it.

It was Chowderhead's sneeze.

*

Chowderhead. Marvin T. Roebuck, his name was. Five feet eight inches tall. Dark-complected, with a cast in one eye. Spoke with a Midwest kind of accent, even though he came from California—"shrick" for "shriek," "hawror" for "horror," like that. It drove me crazy after a while. Maybe that gives you an idea what he talked about mostly. A skunk. A thoroughgoing, deep-rooted, mother-murdering skunk.

I kicked over my chair and roared, "Roebuck! Where are you, damn you?"

The bar was all at once silent. Only the jukebox kept going.

"I know you're here!" I screamed. "Come out and get it! You louse, I told you I'd get you for calling me a liar the day Wally sneaked a smoke!"

Silence, everybody looking at me.

Then the door of the men's room opened.

He came out.

He looked *lousy.* Eyes all red-rimmed and his hair falling out—the poor crumb couldn't have been over twenty-nine. He shrieked, "You!" He called me a million names. He said, "You thieving rat, I'll teach you to try to cheat me out of my candy ration!"

He had a knife.

I didn't care. I didn't have anything and that was stupid, but it didn't matter. I got a bottle of beer from the next table and smashed it against the back of a chair. It made a good weapon, you know; I'd take that against a knife any time.

I ran toward him, and he came all staggering and lurching toward me, looking crazy and desperate, mumbling and raving—I could hardly hear him, because I was talking, too. Nobody tried to stop us. Somebody went out the door and I figured it was to call the cops, but that was all right. Once I took care of Chowderhead, I didn't care what the cops did.

I went for the face.

He cut me first. I felt the knife slide up along my left arm but, you know, it didn't even hurt, only kind of stung a little. I didn't care about that. I got him in the face, and the bottle came away, and it was all like gray and white jelly, and then blood began to spring out. He screamed. Oh, that scream! I never heard anything like that scream. It was what I had been waiting all my life for.

I kicked him as he staggered back, and he fell. And I was on top of him, with the bottle, and I was careful to stay away from the heart or the throat, because that was too quick, but I worked over the face, and I felt his knife get me a couple times more, and—

And—

*

And I woke up, you know. And there was Dr. Santly over me with a hypodermic needle that he'd just taken out of my arm, and four male nurses in fatigues holding me down. And I was drenched with sweat.

For a minute, I didn't know where I was. It was a horrible queasy falling sensation, as though the bar and the fight and the world were all dissolving into smoke around me.

Then I knew where I was.

It was almost worse.

I stopped yelling and just lay there, looking up at them.

Dr. Santly said, trying to keep his face friendly and noncommittal, "You're doing much better, Byron, boy. *Much* better."

I didn't say anything.

He said, "You worked through the whole thing in two hours and eight minutes. Remember the first time? You were sixteen hours killing him. Captain Van Wyck it was that time, remember? Who was it this time?"

"Chowderhead." I looked at the male nurses. Doubtfully, they let go of my arms and legs.

"Chowderhead," said Dr. Santly. "Oh—Roebuck. That boy," he said mournfully, his expression saddened, "he's not coming along nearly as well as you. *Nearly*. He can't run through a cycle in less than five hours. And, that's peculiar, it's usually you he— Well, I better not say that, shall I? No sense setting up a counter-impression when your pores are all open, so to speak?" He smiled at me, but he was a little worried in back of the smile.

I sat up. "Anybody got a cigarette?"

"Give him a cigarette, Johnson," the doctor ordered the male nurse standing alongside my right foot.

Johnson did. I fired up.

"You're coming along *splendidly*," Dr. Santly said. He was one of these psych guys that thinks if you say it's so, it makes it so. You know that kind? "We'll have you down under an hour before the end of the week. That's *marvelous* progress. Then we can work on the conscious level! You're doing extremely well, whether you know it or not. Why, in six months—say in eight months, because I like to be conservative—" he twinkled at me—"we'll have you out of here! You'll be the first of your crew to be discharged, you know that?"

"That's nice," I said. "The others aren't doing so well?"

"No. Not at all well, most of them. Particularly Dr. Gilvey. The run-throughs leave him in terrible shape. I don't mind admitting I'm worried about him."

"That's nice," I said, and this time I meant it.

*

He looked at me thoughtfully, but all he did was say to the male nurses, "He's all right now. Help him off the table."

It was hard standing up. I had to hold onto the rail around the table for a minute. I said my set little speech: "Dr. Santly, I want to tell you again how grateful I am for this. I was reconciled to living the rest of my life confined to one part of the country, the way the other crews always did. But this is much better. I appreciate it. I'm sure the others do, too."

"Of course, boy. Of course." He took out a fountain pen and made a note on my chart; I couldn't see what it was, but he looked gratified. "It's no more than you have coming to you, Byron," he said. "I'm grateful that I could be the one to make it come to pass."

He glanced conspiratorially at the male nurses. "You know how important this is to me. It's the triumph of a whole new approach to psychic rehabilitation. I mean to say our heroes of space travel are entitled to freedom when they come back home to Earth, aren't they?"

"Definitely," I said, scrubbing some of the sweat off my face onto my sleeve.

"So we've got to end this system of designated areas. We can't avoid the tensions that accompany space travel, no. But if we can help you eliminate harmful tensions with a few run-throughs, why, it's not too high a price to pay, is it?"

"Not a bit."

"I mean to say," he said, warming up, "you can look forward to the time when you'll be able to mingle with your old friends from the rocket, free and easy, without any need for restraint. That's a lot to look forward to, isn't it?"

"It is," I said. "I look forward to it very much," I said. "And I know exactly what I'm going to do the first time I meet one—I mean without any restraints, as you say," I said. And it was true; I did. Only it wouldn't be a broken beer bottle that I would do it with.

I had much more elaborate ideas than that.

PYTHIAS

Sure, Larry Connaught saved my life—but it was how he did it that forced me to murder him!

I am sitting on the edge of what passes for a bed. It is made of loosely woven strips of steel, and there is no mattress, only an extra blanket of thin olive-drab. It isn't comfortable; but of course they expect to make me still more uncomfortable.

They expect to take me out of this precinct jail to the District prison and eventually to the death house.

Sure, there will be a trial first, but that is only a formality. Not only did they catch me with the smoking gun in my hand and Connaught bubbling to death through the hole in his throat, but I admitted it.

I—knowing what I was doing, with, as they say, malice aforethought—deliberately shot to death Laurence Connaught. They execute murderers. So they mean to execute me.

Especially because Laurence Connaught had saved my life.

Well, there are extenuating circumstances. I do not think they would convince a jury.

Connaught and I were close friends for years. We lost touch during the war. We met again in Washington, a few years after the war was over. We had, to some extent, grown apart; he had become a man with a mission. He was working very hard on something and he did not choose to discuss his work and there was nothing else in his life on which to form a basis for communication. And—well, I had my own life, too. It wasn't scientific research in my case—I flunked out of med school, while he went on. I'm not ashamed of it; it is nothing to be ashamed of. I simply was not able to cope with the messy business of carving corpses. I didn't like it, I didn't want to do it, and when I was forced to do it, I did it badly. So—I left.

Thus I have no string of degrees, but you don't need them in order to be a Senate guard.

*

Does that sound like a terribly impressive career to you? Of course not; but I liked it. The Senators are relaxed and friendly when the

78 Frederik Pohl

guards are around, and you learn wonderful things about what goes on behind the scenes of government. And a Senate guard is in a position to do favors—for newspapermen, who find a lead to a story useful; for government officials, who sometimes base a whole campaign on one careless, repeated remark; and for just about anyone who would like to be in the visitors' gallery during a hot debate.

Larry Connaught, for instance. I ran into him on the street one day, and we chatted for a moment, and he asked if it was possible to get him in to see the upcoming foreign relations debate. It was; I called him the next day and told him I had arranged for a pass. And he was there, watching eagerly with his moist little eyes, when the Secretary got up to speak and there was that sudden unexpected yell, and the handful of Central American fanatics dragged out their weapons and began trying to change American policy with gunpowder.

You remember the story, I suppose. There were only three of them, two with guns, one with a hand grenade. The pistol men managed to wound two Senators and a guard. I was right there, talking to Connaught. I spotted the little fellow with the hand grenade and tackled him. I knocked him down, but the grenade went flying, pin pulled, seconds ticking away. I lunged for it. Larry Connaught was ahead of me.

The newspaper stories made heroes out of both of us. They said it was miraculous that Larry, who had fallen right on top of the grenade, had managed to get it away from himself and so placed that when it exploded no one was hurt.

For it did go off—and the flying steel touched nobody. The papers mentioned that Larry had been knocked unconscious by the blast. He was unconscious, all right.

He didn't come to for six hours and when he woke up, he spent the next whole day in a stupor.

I called on him the next night. He was glad to see me.

"That was a close one, Dick," he said. "Take me back to Tarawa."

I said, "I guess you saved my life, Larry."

"Nonsense, Dick! I just jumped. Lucky, that's all."

"The papers said you were terrific. They said you moved so fast, nobody could see exactly what happened."

He made a deprecating gesture, but his wet little eyes were wary. "Nobody was really watching, I suppose."

"I was watching," I told him flatly.

He looked at me silently for a moment.

"I was between you and the grenade," I said. "You didn't go past me, over me, or through me. But you were on top of the grenade."

He started to shake his head.

I said, "Also, Larry, you fell *on* the grenade. It exploded underneath you. I know, because I was almost on top of you, and it blew you clear off the floor of the gallery. Did you have a bulletproof vest on?"

*

He cleared his throat. "Well, as a matter of—"

"Cut it out, Larry! What's the answer?"

He took off his glasses and rubbed his watery eyes. He grumbled, "Don't you read the papers? It went off a yard away."

"Larry," I said gently, "I was there."

He slumped back in his chair, staring at me. Larry Connaught was a small man, but he never looked smaller than he did in that big chair, looking at me as though I were Mr. Nemesis himself.

Then he laughed. He surprised me; he sounded almost happy. He said, "Well, hell, Dick—I had to tell somebody about it sooner or later. Why not you?"

I can't tell you all of what he said. I'll tell most of it—but not the part that matters.

I'll never tell *that* part to *anybody*.

Larry said, "I should have known you'd remember." He smiled at me ruefully, affectionately. "Those bull sessions in the cafeterias, eh? Talking all night about everything. But you remembered."

"You claimed that the human mind possessed powers of psychokinesis," I said. "You argued that just by the mind, without moving a finger or using a machine, a man could move his body anywhere, instantly. You said that nothing was impossible to the mind."

I felt like an absolute fool saying those things; they were ridiculous notions. Imagine a man *thinking* himself from one place to another! But—I had been on that gallery.

I licked my lips and looked to Larry Connaught for confirmation.

"I was all wet," Larry laughed. "Imagine!"

I suppose I showed surprise, because he patted my shoulder.

He said, becoming sober, "Sure, Dick, you're wrong, but you're right all the same. The mind alone can't do anything of the sort—that was just a silly kid notion. But," he went on, "*but* there are—well, techniques—linking the mind to physical forces—simple physical forces that we all use every day—that can do it all. Everything! Everything I ever thought of and things I haven't found out yet.

"Fly across the ocean? In a second, Dick! Wall off an exploding bomb? Easily! You saw me do it. Oh, it's work. It takes energy—you can't escape natural law. That was what knocked me out for a whole day. But that was a hard one; it's a lot easier, for instance, to make a bullet miss its target. It's even easier to lift the cartridge out of the chamber and put it in my pocket, so that the bullet can't even be fired. Want the Crown Jewels of England? I could get them, Dick!"

I asked, "Can you see the future?"

He frowned. "That's silly. This isn't supersti—"

"How about reading minds?"

*

Larry's expression cleared. "Oh, you're remembering some of the things I said years ago. No, I can't do that either, Dick. Maybe, some day, if I keep working at this thing— Well, I can't right now. There are things I can do, though, that are just as good."

"Show me something you can do," I asked.

He smiled. Larry was enjoying himself; I didn't begrudge it to him. He had hugged this to himself for years, from the day he found his first clue, through the decade of proving and experimenting, almost always being wrong, but always getting closer.... He *needed* to talk about it. I think he was really glad that, at last, someone had found him out.

He said, "Show you something? Why, let's see, Dick." He looked around the room, then winked. "See that window?"

I looked. It opened with a slither of wood and a rumble of sash weights. It closed again.

"The radio," said Larry. There was a *click* and his little set turned itself on. "Watch it."

It disappeared and reappeared.

"It was on top of Mount Everest," Larry said, panting a little.

The plug on the radio's electric cord picked itself up and stretched toward the baseboard socket, then dropped to the floor again.

"No," said Larry, and his voice was trembling, "I'll show you a hard one. Watch the radio, Dick. I'll run it without plugging it in! The electrons themselves—"

He was staring intently at the little set. I saw the dial light go on, flicker, and hold steady; the speaker began to make scratching noises. I stood up, right behind Larry, right over him.

I used the telephone on the table beside him. I caught him right beside the ear and he folded over without a murmur. Methodically, I hit him twice more, and then I was sure he wouldn't wake up for at least an hour. I rolled him over and put the telephone back in its cradle.

I ransacked his apartment. I found it in his desk: All his notes. All the information. The secret of how to do the things he could do.

I picked up the telephone and called the Washington police. When I heard the siren outside, I took out my service revolver and shot him in the throat. He was dead before they came in.

*

For, you see, I knew Laurence Connaught. We were friends. I would have trusted him with my life. But this was more than just a life.

Twenty-three words told how to do the things that Laurence Connaught did. Anyone who could read could do them. Criminals, traitors, lunatics—the formula would work for anyone.

Laurence Connaught was an honest man and an idealist, I think. But what would happen to any man when he became God? Suppose you were told twenty-three words that would let you reach into any bank vault, peer inside any closed room, walk through any wall? Suppose pistols could not kill you?

They say power corrupts; and absolute power corrupts absolutely. And there can be no more absolute power than the twenty-three words that can free a man of any jail or give him anything he wants. Larry was my friend. But I killed him in cold blood, knowing what I did, because he could not be trusted with the secret that could make him king of the world.

But I can.

THE KNIGHTS OF ARTHUR

TABLE OF CONTENTS

I

There was three of us—I mean if you count Arthur. We split up to avoid attracting attention. Engdahl just came in over the big bridge, but I had Arthur with me so I had to come the long way around.

When I registered at the desk, I said I was from Chicago. You know how it is. If you say you're from Philadelphia, it's like saying you're from St. Louis or Detroit—I mean *nobody* lives in Philadelphia any more. Shows how things change. A couple years ago, Philadelphia was all the fashion. But not now, and I wanted to make a good impression.

I even tipped the bellboy a hundred and fifty dollars. I said: "Do me a favor. I've got my baggage booby-trapped—"

"Natch," he said, only mildly impressed by the bill and a half, even less impressed by me.

"I mean *really* booby-trapped. Not just a burglar alarm. Besides the alarm, there's a little surprise on a short fuse. So what I want you to do, if you hear the alarm go off, is come running. Right?"

"And get my head blown off?" He slammed my bags onto the floor. "Mister, you can take your damn money and—"

"Wait a minute, friend." I passed over another hundred. "Please? It's only a shaped charge. It won't hurt anything except anybody who messes around, see? But I don't want it to go off. So you come running when you hear the alarm and scare him away and—"

"No!" But he was less positive. I gave him two hundred more and he said grudgingly: "All right. If I hear it. Say, what's in there that's worth all that trouble?"

"Papers," I lied.

He leered. "Sure."

"No fooling, it's just personal stuff. Not worth a penny to anybody but me, understand? So don't get any ideas—"

He said in an injured tone: "Mister, naturally the *staff* won't bother your stuff. What kind of a hotel do you think this is?"

"Of course, of course," I said. But I knew he was lying, because I knew what kind of hotel it was. The staff was there only because being there gave them a chance to knock down more money than they could make any other way. What other kind of hotel was there?

Anyway, the way to keep the staff on my side was by bribery, and when he left I figured I had him at least temporarily bought. He promised to keep an eye on the room and he would be on duty for four more hours—which gave me plenty of time for my errands.

*

I made sure Arthur was plugged in and cleaned myself up. They had water running—New York's very good that way; they always have water running. It was even hot, or nearly hot. I let the shower splash over me for a while, because there was a lot of dust and dirt from the Bronx that I had to get off me. The way it looked, hardly anybody had been up that way since it happened.

I dried myself, got dressed and looked out the window. We were fairly high up—fifteenth floor. I could see the Hudson and the big bridge up north of us. There was a huge cloud of smoke coming from somewhere near the bridge on the other side of the river, but outside of that everything looked normal. You would have thought there were people in all those houses. Even the streets looked pretty good, until you noticed that hardly any of the cars were moving.

I opened the little bag and loaded my pockets with enough money to run my errands. At the door, I stopped and called over my shoulder to Arthur: "Don't worry if I'm gone an hour or so. I'll be back."

I didn't wait for an answer. That would have been pointless under the circumstances.

After Philadelphia, this place seemed to be bustling with activity. There were four or five people in the lobby and a couple of dozen more out in the street.

I tarried at the desk for several reasons. In the first place, I was expecting Vern Engdahl to try to contact me and I didn't want him messing with the luggage—not while Arthur might get nervous. So I told the desk clerk that in case anybody came inquiring for Mr. Schlaepfer, which was the name I was using—my real name being Sam Dunlap—he was to be told that on no account was he to go to my room but to wait in the lobby; and in any case I would be back in an hour.

"Sure," said the desk clerk, holding out his hand.

I crossed it with paper. "One other thing," I said. "I need to buy an electric typewriter and some other stuff. Where can I get them?"

"PX," he said promptly.

"PX?"

"What used to be Macy's," he explained. "You go out that door and turn right. It's only about a block. You'll see the sign."

"Thanks." That cost me a hundred more, but it was worth it. After all, money wasn't a problem—not when we had just come from Philadelphia.

*

The big sign read "PX," but it wasn't big enough to hide an older sign underneath that said "Macy's." I looked it over from across the street.

Somebody had organized it pretty well. I had to admire them. I mean I don't like New York—wouldn't live there if you gave me the place—but it showed a sort of go-getting spirit. It was no easy job getting a full staff together to run a department store operation, when any city the size of New York must have a couple thousand stores. You know what I mean? It's like running a hotel or anything else—how are you going to get people to work for you when they can just as easily walk down the street, find a vacant store and set up their own operation?

But Macy's was fully manned. There was a guard at every door and a walking patrol along the block-front between the entrances to make sure nobody broke in through the windows. They all wore green armbands and uniforms—well, lots of people wore uniforms.

I walked over.

"Afternoon," I said affably to the guard. "I want to pick up some stuff. Typewriter, maybe a gun, you know. How do you work it here? Flat rate for all you can carry, prices marked on everything, or what is it?"

He stared at me suspiciously. He was a monster; six inches taller than I, he must have weighed two hundred and fifty pounds. He didn't look very smart, which might explain why he was working for somebody else these days. But he was smart enough for what he had to do.

He demanded: "You new in town?"

I nodded.

He thought for a minute. "All right, buddy. Go on in. You pick out what you want, see? We'll straighten out the price when you come out."

"Fair enough." I started past him.

He grabbed me by the arm. "No tricks," he ordered. "You come out the same door you went in, understand?"

"Sure," I said, "if that's the way you want it."

That figured—one way or another: either they got a commission, or, like everybody else, they lived on what they could knock down. I filed that for further consideration.

Inside, the store smelled pretty bad. It wasn't just rot, though there was plenty of that; it was musty and stale and old. It was dark, or nearly. About one light in twenty was turned on, in order to conserve power. Naturally the escalators and so on weren't running at all.

*

I passed a counter with pencils and ball-point pens in a case. Most of them were gone—somebody hadn't bothered to go around in back and had simply knocked the glass out—but I found one that worked and an old order pad to write on. Over by the elevators there was a store directory, so I went over and checked it, making a list of the departments worth visiting.

Office Supplies would be the typewriter. Garden & Home was a good bet—maybe I could find a little wheelbarrow to save carrying the typewriter in my arms. What I wanted was one of the big ones where all the keys are solenoid-operated instead of the cam-and-roller arrangement—that was all Arthur could operate. And those things were heavy, as I knew. That was why we had ditched the old one in the Bronx.

Sporting Goods—that would be for a gun, if there were any left. Naturally, they were about the first to go after it happened, when *everybody* wanted a gun. I mean everybody who lived through it. I thought about clothes—it was pretty hot in New York—and decided I might as well take a look.

Typewriter, clothes, gun, wheelbarrow. I made one more note on the pad—try the tobacco counter, but I didn't have much hope for that. They had used cigarettes for currency around this area for a while, until they got enough bank vaults open to supply big bills. It made cigarettes scarce.

I turned away and noticed for the first time that one of the elevators was stopped on the main floor. The doors were closed, but they were glass doors, and although there wasn't any light inside, I could see the elevator was full. There must have been thirty or forty people in the car when it happened.

I'd been thinking that, if nothing else, these New Yorkers were pretty neat—I mean if you don't count the Bronx. But here were thirty or forty skeletons that nobody had even bothered to clear away.

You call that neat? Right in plain view on the ground floor, where everybody who came into the place would be sure to go—I mean if it had been on one of the upper floors, what difference would it have made?

I began to wish we were out of the city. But naturally that would have to wait until we finished what we came here to do—otherwise, what was the point of coming all the way here in the first place?

*

The tobacco counter was bare. I got the wheelbarrow easily enough—there were plenty of those, all sizes; I picked out a nice light red-and-yellow one with rubber-tired wheel. I rolled it over to Sporting Goods on the same floor, but that didn't work out too well. I found a 30-30 with telescopic sights, only there weren't any cartridges to fit it—or anything else. I took the gun anyway; Engdahl would probably have some extra ammunition.

Men's Clothing was a waste of time, too—I guess these New Yorkers were too lazy to do laundry. But I found the typewriter I wanted.

I put the whole load into the wheelbarrow, along with a couple of odds and ends that caught my eye as I passed through Housewares, and I bumped as gently as I could down the shallow steps of the motionless escalator to the ground floor.

I came down the back way, and that was a mistake. It led me right past the food department. Well, I don't have to tell you what *that* was like, with all the exploded cans and the rats as big as poodles. But I found some cologne and soaked a handkerchief in it, and with that over my nose, and some fast footwork for the rats, I managed to get to one of the doors.

It wasn't the one I had come in, but that was all right. I sized up the guard. He looked smart enough for a little bargaining, but not too smart; and if I didn't like his price, I could always remember that I was supposed to go out the other door.

I said: "Psst!"

When he turned around, I said rapidly: "Listen, this isn't the way I came in, but if you want to do business, it'll be the way I come out."

He thought for a second, and then he smiled craftily and said: "All right, come on."

Well, we haggled. The gun was the big thing—he wanted five thousand for that and he wouldn't come down. The wheelbarrow he was willing to let go for five hundred. And the typewriter—he scowled at the typewriter as though it were contagious.

"What you want that for?" he asked suspiciously. I shrugged.

"Well—" he scratched his head—"a thousand?"

I shook my head.

"Five hundred?"

I kept on shaking.

"All right, all right," he grumbled. "Look, you take the other things for six thousand—including what you got in your pockets that you don't think I know about, see? And I'll throw this in. How about it?"

That was fine as far as I was concerned, but just on principle I pushed him a little further. "Forget it," I said. "I'll give you fifty bills for the lot, take it or leave it. Otherwise I'll walk right down the street to Gimbel's and—"

He guffawed.

"Whats the matter?" I demanded.

"Pal," he said, "you kill me. Stranger in town, hey? You can't go anyplace but here."

"Why not?"

"Account of there *ain't* anyplace else. See, the chief here don't like competition. So we don't have to worry about anybody taking their trade elsewhere, like—we burned all the other places down."

That explained a couple of things. I counted out the money, loaded the stuff back in the wheelbarrow and headed for the Statler; but all the time I was counting and loading, I was talking to Big Brainless; and by the time I was actually on the way, I knew a little more about this "chief."

And that was kind of important, because he was the man we were going to have to know very well.

II

I locked the door of the hotel room. Arthur was peeping out of the suitcase at me.

I said: "I'm back. I got your typewriter." He waved his eye at me.

I took out the little kit of electricians' tools I carried, tipped the typewriter on its back and began sorting out leads. I cut them free from the keyboard, soldered on a ground wire, and began taping the leads to the strands of a yard of forty-ply multiplex cable.

It was a slow and dull job. I didn't have to worry about which solenoid lead went to which strand—Arthur could sort them out. But all the same it took an hour, pretty near, and I was getting hungry by the time I got the last connection taped. I shifted the typewriter so that both Arthur and I could see it, rolled in a sheet of paper and hooked the cable to Arthur's receptors.

Nothing happened.

"Oh," I said. "Excuse me, Arthur. I forgot to plug it in."

I found a wall socket. The typewriter began to hum and then it started to rattle and type:

DURA AUK UKOO RQK MWS AQB

It stopped.

"Come on, Arthur," I ordered impatiently. "Sort them out, will you?"

Laboriously it typed:

!!!

Then, for a time, there was a clacking and thumping as he typed random letters, peeping out of the suitcase to see what he had typed, until the sheet I had put in was used up.

I replaced it and waited, as patiently as I could, smoking one of the last of my cigarettes. After fifteen minutes or so, he had the hang of it pretty well. He typed:

YOU DAMQXXX DAMN FOOL WHUXXX WHY DID YOU LEAQNXXX LEAVE ME ALONE Q Q

"Aw, Arthur," I said. "Use your head, will you? I couldn't carry that old typewriter of yours all the way down through the Bronx. It was getting pretty beat-up. Anyway, I've only got two hands—"

YOU LOUSE, it rattled, ARE YOU TRYONXXX TRYING TO INSULT ME BECAUSE I DONT HAVE ANY Q Q

"Arthur!" I said, shocked. "You know better than that!"

The typewriter slammed its carriage back and forth ferociously a couple of times. Then he said: ALL RIGHT SAM YOU KNOW YOUVE GOT ME BY THE THROAT SO YOU CAN DO ANYTHING YOU WANT TO WITH ME WHO CARES ABOUT MY FEELINGS ANYHOW

"Please don't take that attitude," I coaxed.

WELL

"Please?"

He capitulated. ALL RIGHT SAY HEARD ANYTHING FROM ENGDAHL Q Q

"No."

ISNT THAT JUST LIKE HIM Q Q CANT DEPEND ON THAT MAN HE WAS THE LOUSIEST ELECTRICIANS MATE ON THE SEA SPRITE AND HE ISNT MUCH BETTER NOW SAY SAM REMEMBER WHEN WE HAD TO GET HIM OUT OF THE JUG IN NEWPORT NEWS BECAUSE

I settled back and relaxed. I might as well. That was the trouble with getting Arthur a new typewriter after a couple of days without one—he had so much garrulity stored up in his little brain, and the only person to spill it on was me.

*

Apparently I fell asleep. Well, I mean I must have, because I woke up. I had been dreaming I was on guard post outside the Yard at Portsmouth, and it was night, and I looked up and there was something up there, all silvery and bad. It was a missile—and that was silly, because you never see a missile. But this was a dream.

And the thing burst, like a Roman candle flaring out, all sorts of comet-trails of light, and then the whole sky was full of bright and colored snow. Little tiny flakes of light coming down, a mist of light, radiation dropping like dew; and it was so pretty, and I took a deep breath. And my lungs burned out like slow fire, and I coughed myself to death with the explosions of the missile banging against my flaming ears. . . .

Well, it was a dream. It probably wasn't like that at all—and if it had been, I wasn't there to see it, because I was tucked away safe under a hundred and twenty fathoms of Atlantic water. All of us were on the *Sea Sprite*.

But it was a bad dream and it bothered me, even when I woke up and found that the banging explosions of the missile were the noise of Arthur's typewriter carriage crashing furiously back and forth.

He peeped out of the suitcase and saw that I was awake. He demanded: HOW CAN YOU FALL ASLEEP WHEN WERE IN A PLACE LIKE THIS Q Q ANYTHING COULD HAPPEN SAM I KNOW YOU DONT CARE WHAT HAPPENS TO ME BUT FOR YOUR OWN SAKE YOU SHOULDNT

"Oh, dry up," I said.

Being awake, I remembered that I was hungry. There was still no sign of Engdahl or the others, but that wasn't too surprising—they hadn't known exactly when we would arrive. I wished I had thought to bring some food back to the room. It looked like long waiting and I wouldn't want to leave Arthur alone again—after all, he was partly right.

I thought of the telephone.

On the off-chance that it might work, I picked it up. Amazing, a voice from the desk answered.

I crossed my fingers and said: "Room service?"

And the voice answered amiably enough: "Hold on, buddy. I'll see if they answer."

Clicking and a good long wait. Then a new voice said: "Whaddya want?"

There was no sense pressing my luck by asking for anything like a complete meal. I would be lucky if I got a sandwich.

I said: "Please, may I have a Spam sandwich on Rye Krisp and some coffee for Room Fifteen Forty-one?"

"Please, you go to hell!" the voice snarled. "What do you think this is, some damn delicatessen? You want liquor, we'll get you liquor. That's what room service is for!"

*

I hung up. What was the use of arguing? Arthur was clacking peevishly:

WHATS THE MATTER SAM YOU THINKING OF YOUR BELLY AGAIN Q Q

"You would be if you—" I started, and then I stopped. Arthur's feelings were delicate enough already. I mean suppose that all you had left of what you were born with was a brain in a kind of sardine can, wouldn't you be sensitive? Well, Arthur was more sensitive than you would be, believe me. Of course, it was his own foolish fault—I mean you don't get a prosthetic tank unless you die by accident, or something like that, because if it's disease they usually can't save even the brain.

The phone rang again.

It was the desk clerk. "Say, did you get what you wanted?" he asked chummily.

"No."

"Oh. Too bad," he said, but cheerfully. "Listen, buddy, I forgot to tell you before. That Miss Engdahl you were expecting, she's on her way up."

I dropped the phone onto the cradle.

"Arthur!" I yelled. "Keep quiet for a while—trouble!"

He clacked once, and the typewriter shut itself off. I jumped for the door of the bathroom, cursing the fact that I didn't have cartridges for the gun. Still, empty or not, it would have to do.

I ducked behind the bathroom door, in the shadows, covering the hall door. Because there were two things wrong with what the desk clerk had told me. Vern Engdahl wasn't a "miss," to begin with; and whatever name he used when he came to call on me, it wouldn't be Vern Engdahl.

There was a knock on the door. I called: "Come in!"

The door opened and the girl who called herself Vern Engdahl came in slowly, looking around. I stayed quiet and out of sight until she was all the way in. She didn't seem to be armed; there wasn't anyone with her.

I stepped out, holding the gun on her. Her eyes opened wide and she seemed about to turn.

"Hold it! Come on in, you. Close the door!"

She did. She looked as though she were expecting me. I looked her over—medium pretty, not very tall, not very plump, not very old. I'd have guessed twenty or so, but that's not my line of work; she could have been almost any age from seventeen on.

The typewriter switched itself on and began to pound agitatedly. I crossed over toward her and paused to peer at what Arthur was yacking about: SEARCH HER YOU DAMN FOOL MAYBE SHES GOT A GUN

I ordered: "Shut up, Arthur. I'm *going* to search her. You! Turn around!"

*

She shrugged and turned around, her hands in the air. Over her shoulder, she said: "You're taking this all wrong, Sam. I came here to make a deal with you."

"Sure you did."

But her knowing my name was a blow, too. I mean what was the use of all that sneaking around if people in New York were going to know we were here?

I walked up close behind her and patted what there was to pat. There didn't seem to be a gun.

"You tickle," she complained.

I took her pocketbook away from her and went through it. No gun. A lot of money—an *awful* lot of money. I mean there must have been two or three hundred thousand dollars. There was nothing with a name on it in the pocketbook.

She said: "Can I put my hands down, Sam?"

"In a minute." I thought for a second and then decided to do it—you know, I just couldn't afford to take chances. I cleared my throat and ordered: "Take off your clothes."

Her head jerked around and she stared at me. "*What?*"

"Take them off. You heard me."

"Now wait a minute—" she began dangerously.

I said: "Do what I tell you, hear? How do I know you haven't got a knife tucked away?"

She clenched her teeth. "Why, you dirty little man! What do you think—" Then she shrugged. She looked at me with contempt and said: "All right. What's the difference?"

Well, there was a considerable difference. She began to unzip and unbutton and wriggle, and pretty soon she was standing there in her underwear, looking at me as though I were a two-headed worm. It was interesting, but kind of embarrassing. I could see Arthur's eye-stalk waving excitedly out of the opened suitcase.

I picked up her skirt and blouse and shook them. I could feel myself blushing, and there didn't seem to be anything in them.

I growled: "Okay, I guess that's enough. You can put your clothes back on now."

"Gee, thanks," she said.

She looked at me thoughtfully and then shook her head as if she'd never seen anything like me before and never hoped to again.

Without another word, she began to get back into her clothes. I had to admire her poise. I mean she was perfectly calm about the whole thing. You'd have thought she was used to taking her clothes off in front of strange men.

Well, for that matter, maybe she was; but it wasn't any of my business.

*

Arthur was clacking distractedly, but I didn't pay any attention to him. I demanded: "All right, now who are you and what do you want?"

She pulled up a stocking and said: "You couldn't have asked me that in the first place, could you? I'm Vern Eng—"

"*Cut it out!*"

She stared at me. "I was only going to say I'm Vern Engdahl's partner. We've got a little business deal cooking and I wanted to talk to you about this proposition."

Arthur squawked: WHATS ENGDAHL UP TO NOW Q Q SAM IM WARNING YOU I DONT LIKE THE LOOK OF THIS THIS WOMAN AND ENGDAHL ARE PROBABLY DOUBLECROSSING US

I said: "All right, Arthur, relax. I'm taking care of things. Now start over, you. What's your name?"

She finished putting on her shoe and stood up. "Amy."

"Last name?"

She shrugged and fished in her purse for a cigarette. "What does it matter? Mind if I sit down?"

"Go ahead," I rumbled. "But don't stop talking!"

"Oh," she said, "we've got plenty of time to straighten things out." She lit the cigarette and walked over to the chair by the window. On the way, she gave the luggage a good long look.

Arthur's eyestalk cowered back into the suitcase as she came close. She winked at me, grinned, bent down and peered inside.

"My," she said, "he's a nice shiny one, isn't he?"

The typewriter began to clatter frantically. I didn't even bother to look; I told him: "Arthur, if you can't keep quiet, you have to expect people to know you're there."

She sat down and crossed her legs. "Now then," she said. "Frankly, he's what I came to see you about. Vern told me you had a pross. I want to buy it."

The typewriter thrashed its carriage back and forth furiously.

"Arthur isn't for sale."

"No?" She leaned back. "Vern's already sold me his interest, you know. And you don't really have any choice. You see, I'm in charge of materiel procurement for the Major. If you want to sell your share, fine. If you don't, why, we requisition it anyhow. Do you follow?"

I was getting irritated—at Vern Engdahl, for whatever the hell he thought he was doing; but at her because she was handy. I shook my head.

"Fifty thousand dollars? I mean for your interest?"

"No."

"Seventy-five?"

"No!"

"Oh, come on now. A hundred thousand?"

It wasn't going to make any impression on her, but I tried to explain: "Arthur's a friend of mine. He isn't for sale."

*

She shook her head. "What's the matter with you? Engdahl wasn't like this. He sold his interest for forty thousand and was glad to get it."

Clatter-clatter-clatter from Arthur. I didn't blame him for having hurt feelings that time.

Amy said in a discouraged tone: "Why can't people be reasonable? The Major doesn't like it when people aren't reasonable."

I lowered the gun and cleared my throat. "He doesn't?" I asked, cuing her. I wanted to hear more about this Major, who seemed to have the city pretty well under his thumb.

"No, he doesn't." She shook her head sorrowfully. She said in an accusing voice: "You out-of-towners don't know what it's like to try to run a city the size of New York. There are fifteen thousand people here, do you know that? It isn't one of your hick towns. And it's worry, worry, worry all the time, trying to keep things going."

"I bet," I said sympathetically. "You're, uh, pretty close to the Major?"

She said stiffly: "I'm not married to him, if that's what you mean. Though I've had my chances. . . . But you see how it is. Fifteen thousand people to run a place the size of New York! It's forty men to operate the power station, and twenty-five on the PX, and thirty on the hotel here. And then there are the local groceries, and the Army, and the Coast Guard, and the Air Force—though, really, that's only two men—and—Well, you get the picture."

"I certainly do. Look, what kind of a guy *is* the Major?"

She shrugged. "A guy."

"I mean what does he like?"

"Women, mostly," she said, her expression clouded. "Come on now. What about it?"

I stalled. "What do you want Arthur for?"

She gave me a disgusted look. "What do you think? To relieve the manpower shortage, naturally. There's more work than there are men. Now if the Major could just get hold of a couple of prosthetics, like this thing here, why, he could put them in the big installations. This one used to be an engineer or something, Vern said."

"Well . . . *like* an engineer."

*

Amy shrugged. "So why couldn't we connect him up with the power station? It's been done. The Major knows that—he was in the Pentagon when they switched all the aircraft warning net over from computer to prosthetic control. So why couldn't we do the same thing with our power station and release forty men for other assignments? This thing could work day, night, Sundays—what's the difference when you're just a brain in a sardine can?"

Clatter-rattle-*bang.*

She looked startled. "Oh. I forgot he was listening."

"No deal," I said.

She said: "A hundred and fifty thousand?"

A hundred and fifty thousand dollars. I considered that for a while. Arthur clattered warningly.

"Well," I temporized, "I'd have to be sure he was getting into good hands—"

The typewriter thrashed wildly. The sheet of paper fluttered out of the carriage. He'd used it up. Automatically I picked it up—it was covered with imprecations, self-pity and threats—and started to put a new one in.

"No," I said, bending over the typewriter, "I guess I couldn't sell him. It just wouldn't be right—"

That was my mistake; it was the wrong time for me to say that, because I had taken my eyes off her.

The room bent over and clouted me.

I half turned, not more than a fraction conscious, and I saw this Amy girl, behind me, with the shoe still in her hand, raised to give me another blackjacking on the skull.

The shoe came down, and it must have weighed more than it looked, and even the fractional bit of consciousness went crashing away.

III

I have to tell you about Vern Engdahl. We were all from the *Sea Sprite*, of course—me and Vern and even Arthur. The thing about Vern is that he was the lowest-ranking one of us all—only an electricians' mate third, I mean when anybody paid any attention to things like that—and yet he was pretty much doing the thinking for the rest of us. Coming to New York was his idea—he told us that was the only place we could get what we wanted.

Well, as long as we were carrying Arthur along with us, we pretty much needed Vern, because he was the one who knew how to keep the lash-up going. You've got no idea what kind of pumps and plumbing go into a prosthetic tank until you've seen one opened up. And, naturally, Arthur didn't want any breakdowns without somebody around to fix things up.

The *Sea Sprite*, maybe you know, was one of the old liquid-sodium-reactor subs—too slow for combat duty, but as big as a barn, so they made it a hospital ship. We were cruising deep when the missiles hit, and, of course, when we came up, there wasn't much for a hospital ship to do. I mean there isn't any sense fooling around with anybody who's taken a good deep breath of fallout.

So we went back to Newport News to see what had happened. And we found out what had happened. And there wasn't anything much to do except pay off the crew and let them go. But us three stuck together. Why not? It wasn't as if we had any families to go back to any more.

Vern just loved all this stuff—he'd been an Eagle Scout; maybe that had something to do with it—and he showed us how to boil drinking water and forage in the woods and all like that, because nobody in his right mind wanted to go near any kind of a town, until the cold weather set in, anyway. And it was always Vern, Vern, telling us what to do, ironing out our troubles.

It worked out, except that there was this one thing. Vern had bright ideas. But he didn't always tell us what they were.

So I wasn't so very surprised when I came to. I mean there I was, tied up, with this girl Amy standing over me, holding the gun like a club. Evidently she'd found out that there weren't any cartridges. And in a couple of minutes there was a knock on the door, and she yelled, "Come in," and in came Vern. And the man who was with him had to be somebody important, because there were eight or ten other men crowding in close behind.

I didn't need to look at the oak leaves on his shoulders to realize that here was the chief, the fellow who ran this town, the Major.

It was just the kind of thing Vern *would* do.

*

Vern said, with the look on his face that made strange officers wonder why this poor persecuted man had been forced to spend so much time in the brig: "Now, Major, I'm sure we can straighten all this out. Would you mind leaving me alone with my friend here for a moment?"

The Major teetered on his heels, thinking. He was a tall, youngish-bald type, with a long, worried, horselike face. He said: "Ah, do you think we should?"

"I guarantee there'll be no trouble, Major," Vern promised.

The Major pulled at his little mustache. "Very well," he said. "Amy, you come along."

"We'll be right here, Major," Vern said reassuringly, escorting him to the door.

"You bet you will," said the Major, and tittered. "Ah, bring that gun along with you, Amy. And be sure this man knows that we have bullets."

They closed the door. Arthur had been cowering in his suitcase, but now his eyestalk peeped out and the rattling and clattering from that typewriter sounded like the Battle of the Bulge.

I demanded: "Come on, Vern. What's this all about?"

Vern said: "How much did they offer you?"

Clatter-bang-BANG. I peeked, and Arthur was saying: WARNED YOU SAM THAT ENGDAHL WAS UP TO TRICKS PLEASE SAM PLEASE PLEASE PLEASE HIT HIM ON THE HEAD KNOCK HIM OUT HE MUST HAVE A GUN SO GET IT AND SHOOT OUR WAY OUT OF HERE

"A hundred and fifty thousand dollars," I said.

Vern looked outraged. "I only got forty!"

Arthur clattered: VERN I APPEAL TO YOUR COMMON DECENCY WERE OLD SHIPMATES VERN REMEMBER ALL THE TIMES I

"Still," Vern mused, "it's all common funds anyway, right? Arthur belongs to both of us."

I DONT DONT DONT REPEAT DONT BELONG TO ANYBODY BUT ME

"That's true," I said grudgingly. "But I carried him, remember."

SAM WHATS THE MATTER WITH YOU Q Q I DONT LIKE THE EXPRESSION ON YOUR FACE LISTEN SAM YOU ARENT

Vern said, "A hundred and fifty thousand, remember."

THINKING OF SELLING

"And of course we couldn't get out of here," Vern pointed out. "They've got us surrounded."

ME TO THESE RATS Q Q SAM VERN PLEASE DONT SCARE ME

*

I said, pointing to the fluttering paper in the rattling machine: "You're worrying our friend."

Vern shrugged impatiently.

I KNEW I SHOULDNT HAVE TRUSTED YOU, Arthur wept. THATS ALL I MEAN TO YOU EH

Vern said: "Well, Sam? Let's take the cash and get this thing over with. After all, he *will* have the best of treatment."

It was a little like selling your sister into white slavery, but what else was there to do? Besides, I kind of trusted Vern.

"All right," I said.

What Arthur said nearly scorched the paper.

Vern helped pack Arthur up for moving. I mean it was just a matter of pulling the plugs out and making sure he had a fresh battery, but Vern wanted to supervise it himself. Because one of the little things Vern had up his sleeve was that he had found a spot for himself on the Major's payroll. He was now the official Prosthetic (Human) Maintenance Department Chief.

The Major said to me: "Ah, Dunlap. What sort of experience have you had?"

"Experience?"

"In the Navy. Your friend Engdahl suggested you might want to join us here."

"Oh. I see what you mean." I shook my head. "Nothing that would do you any good, I'm afraid. I was a yeoman."

"Yeoman?"

"Like a company clerk," I explained. "I mean I kept records and cut orders and made out reports and all like that."

"Company clerk!" The eyes in the long horsy face gleamed. "Ah, you're mistaken, Dunlap! Why, that's *just* what we need. Our morning reports are in foul shape. Foul! Come over to HQ. Lieutenant Bankhead will give you a lift."

"Lieutenant Bankhead?"

I got an elbow in my ribs for that. It was that girl Amy, standing alongside me. "I," she said, "am Lieutenant Bankhead."

Well, I went along with her, leaving Engdahl and Arthur behind. But I must admit I wasn't sure of my reception.

Out in front of the hotel was a whole fleet of cars—three or four of them, at least. There was a big old Cadillac that looked like a gangsters' car—thick glass in the windows, tires that looked like they belonged on a truck. I was willing to bet it was bulletproof and also that it belonged to the Major. I was right both times. There was a little MG with the top down, and a couple of light trucks. Every one of them was painted bright orange, and every one of them had the star-and-bar of the good old United States Army on its side.

It took me back to old times—all but the unmilitary color. Amy led me to the MG and pointed.

"Sit," she said.

I sat. She got in the other side and we were off.

It was a little uncomfortable on account of I wasn't just sure whether I ought to apologize for making her take her clothes off. And then she tramped on the gas of that little car and I didn't think much about being embarrassed or about her black lace lingerie. I was only thinking about one thing—how to stay alive long enough to get out of that car.

IV

See, what we really wanted was an ocean liner.

The rest of us probably would have been happy enough to stay in Lehigh County, but Arthur was getting restless.

He was a terrible responsibility, in a way. I suppose there were a hundred thousand people or so left in the country, and not more than forty or fifty of them were like Arthur—I mean if you want to call a man in a prosthetic tank a "person." But we all did. We'd got pretty used to him. We'd shipped together in the war—and survived together, as a few of the actual fighters did, those who were lucky enough to be underwater or high in the air when the ICBMs landed—and as few civilians did.

I mean there wasn't much chance for surviving, for anybody who happened to be breathing the open air when it happened. I mean you can do just so much about making a "clean" H-bomb, and if you cut out the long-life fission products, the short-life ones get pretty deadly.

Anyway, there wasn't much damage, except of course that everybody was dead. All the surface vessels lost their crews. All the population of the cities were gone. And so then, when Arthur slipped on the gangplank coming into Newport News and broke his fool neck, why, we had the whole staff of the *Sea Sprite* to work on him. I mean what else did the surgeons have to do?

Of course, that was a long time ago.

But we'd stayed together. We headed for the farm country around Allentown, Pennsylvania, because Arthur and Vern Engdahl claimed to know it pretty well. I think maybe they had some hope of finding family or friends, but naturally there wasn't any of that. And when you got into the inland towns, there hadn't been much of an attempt to clean them up. At least the big cities and the ports had been gone over, in some spots anyway, by burial squads. Although when we finally decided to move out and went to Philadelphia—

Well, let's be fair; there had been fighting around there after the big fight. Anyway, that wasn't so very uncommon. That was one of the reasons that for a long time—four or five years, at any rate—we stayed away from big cities.

We holed up in a big farmhouse in Lehigh County. It had its own generator from a little stream, and that took care of Arthur's power needs; and the previous occupants had been just crazy about stashing away food. There was enough to last a century, and that took care of the two of us. We appreciated that. We even took the old folks out and gave them a decent burial. I mean they'd all been in the family car, so we just had to tow it to a gravel pit and push it in.

The place had its own well, with an electric pump and a hot-water system—oh, it was nice. I was sorry to leave but, frankly, Arthur was driving us nuts.

We never could make the television work—maybe there weren't any stations near enough. But we pulled in a couple of radio stations pretty well and Arthur got a big charge out of listening to them—see, he could hear four or five at a time and I suppose that made him feel better than the rest of us.

He heard that the big cities were cleaned up and every one of them seemed to want immigrants—they were pleading, pleading all the time, like the TV-set and vacuum-cleaner people used to in the old days; they guaranteed we'd like it if we only came to live in Philly, or Richmond, or Baltimore, or wherever. And I guess Arthur kind of hoped we might find another pross. And then—well, Engdahl came up with this idea of an ocean liner.

It figured. I mean you get out in the middle of the ocean and what's the difference what it's like on land? And it especially appealed to Arthur because he wanted to do some surface sailing. He never had when he was real—I mean when he had arms and legs like anybody else. He'd gone right into the undersea service the minute he got out of school.

And—well, sailing was what Arthur knew something about and I suppose even a prosthetic man wants to feel useful. It was like Amy said: He could be hooked up to an automated factory—

Or to a ship.

*

HQ for the Major's Temporary Military Government—that's what
the sign said—was on the 91st floor of the Empire State Building, and
right there that tells you something about the man. I mean you know
how much power it takes to run those elevators all the way up to the
top? But the Major must have liked being able to look down on
everybody else.

Amy Bankhead conducted me to his office and sat me down to wait
for His Military Excellency to arrive. She filled me in on him, to
some degree. He'd been an absolute nothing before the war; but he
had a reserve commission in the Air Force, and when things began
to look sticky, they'd called him up and put him in a Missile Master
control point, underground somewhere up around Ossining.

He was the duty officer when it happened, and naturally he hadn't
noticed anything like an enemy aircraft, and naturally the
anti-missile missiles were still rusting in their racks all around the
city; but since the place had been operating on sealed ventilation, the
duty complement could stay there until the short half-life
radioisotopes wore themselves out.

And then the Major found out that he was not only in charge of
the fourteen men and women of his division at the center—he was
ranking United States Military Establishment officer farther than the
eye could see. So he beat it, fast as he could, for New York, because
what Army officer doesn't dream about being stationed in New York?
And he set up his Temporary Military Government—and that was
nine years ago.

If there hadn't been plenty to go around, I don't suppose he would
have lasted a week—none of these city chiefs would have. But as
things were, he was in on the ground floor, and as newcomers
trickled into the city, his boys already had things nicely organized.

It was a soft touch.

*

Well, we were about a week getting settled in New York and things
were looking pretty good. Vern calmed me down by pointing out

that, after all, we had to sell Arthur, and hadn't we come out of it plenty okay?

And we had. There was no doubt about it. Not only did we have a fat price for Arthur, which was useful because there were a lot of things we would have to buy, but we both had jobs working for the Major.

Vern was his specialist in the care and feeding of Arthur and I was his chief of office routine—and, as such, I delighted his fussy little soul, because by adding what I remembered of Navy protocol to what he was able to teach me of Army routine, we came up with as snarled a mass of red tape as any field-grade officer in the whole history of all armed forces had been able to accumulate. Oh, I tell you, nobody sneezed in New York without a report being made out in triplicate, with eight endorsements.

Of course there wasn't anybody to send them to, but that didn't stop the Major. He said with determination: "Nobody's ever going to chew *me* out for non-compliance with regulations—even if I have to invent the regulations myself!"

We set up in a bachelor apartment on Central Park South—the Major had the penthouse; the whole building had been converted to barracks—and the first chance we got, Vern snaffled some transportation and we set out to find an ocean liner.

See, the thing was that an ocean liner isn't easy to steal. I mean we'd scouted out the lay of the land before we ever entered the city itself, and there were plenty of liners, but there wasn't one that looked like we could just jump in and sail it away. For that we needed an organization. Since we didn't have one, the best thing to do was borrow the Major's.

Vern turned up with Amy Bankhead's MG, and he also turned up with Amy. I can't say I was displeased, because I was beginning to like the girl; but did you ever try to ride three people in the seats of an MG? Well, the way to do it is by having one passenger sit in the other passenger's lap, which would have been all right except that Amy insisted on driving.

We headed downtown and over to the West Side. The Major's Topographical Section—one former billboard artist—had prepared road maps with little red-ink Xs marking the streets that were blocked, which was most of the streets; but we charted a course that would take us where we wanted to go. Thirty-fourth Street was open, and so was Fifth Avenue all of its length, so we scooted down Fifth, crossed over, got under the Elevated Highway and whined along uptown toward the Fifties.

"There's one," cried Amy, pointing.

I was on Vern's lap, so I was making the notes. It was a Fruit Company combination freighter-passenger vessel. I looked at Vern, and Vern shrugged as best he could, so I wrote it down; but it wasn't exactly what we wanted. No, not by a long shot.

*

Still, the thing to do was to survey our resources, and then we could pick the one we liked best. We went all the way up to the end of the big-ship docks, and then turned and came back down, all the way to the Battery. It wasn't pleasure driving, exactly—half a dozen times we had to get out the map and detour around impenetrable jams of stalled and empty cars—or anyway, if they weren't exactly empty, the people in them were no longer in shape to get out of our way. But we made it.

We counted sixteen ships in dock that looked as though they might do for our purposes. We had to rule out the newer ones and the reconverted jobs. I mean, after all, U-235 just lasts so long, and you can steam around the world on a walnut-shell of it, or whatever it is, but you can't store it. So we had to stick with the ships that were powered with conventional fuel—and, on consideration, only oil at that.

But that left sixteen, as I say. Some of them, though, had suffered visibly from being left untended for nearly a decade, so that for our purposes they might as well have been abandoned in the middle of the Atlantic; we didn't have the equipment or ambition to do any great amount of salvage work.

The *Empress of Britain* would have been a pretty good bet, for instance, except that it was lying at pretty nearly a forty-five-degree angle in its berth. So was the *United States*, and so was the *Caronia*. The *Stockholm* was straight enough, but I took a good look, and only one tier of portholes was showing above the water—evidently it had settled nice and even, but it was on the bottom all the same. Well, that mud sucks with a fine tight grip, and we weren't going to try to loosen it.

All in all, eleven of the sixteen ships were out of commission just from what we could see driving by.

Vern and I looked at each other. We stood by the MG, while Amy sprawled her legs over the side and waited for us to make up our minds.

"Not good, Sam," said Vern, looking worried.

I said: "Well, that still leaves five. There's the *Vulcania*, the *Cristobal*—"

"Too small."

"All right. The *Manhattan*, the *Liberté* and the *Queen Elizabeth*."

Amy looked up, her eyes gleaming. "Where's the question?" she demanded. "Naturally, it's the *Queen*."

I tried to explain. "Please, Amy. Leave these things to us, will you?"

"But the Major won't settle for anything but the best!"

"The *Major*?"

*

I glanced at Vern, who wouldn't meet my eyes. "Well," I said, "look at the problems, Amy. First we have to check it over. Maybe it's been burned out—how do we know? Maybe the channel isn't even deep enough to float it any more—how do we know? Where are we going to get the oil for it?"

"We'll get the oil," Amy said cheerfully.

"And what if the channel isn't deep enough?"

"She'll float," Amy promised. "At high tide, anyway. Even if the channel hasn't been dredged in ten years."

I shrugged and gave up. What was the use of arguing?

We drove back to the *Queen Elizabeth* and I had to admit that there was a certain attraction about that big old dowager. We all got out and strolled down the pier, looking over as much as we could see.

The pier had never been cleaned out. It bothered me a little—I mean I don't like skeletons much—but Amy didn't seem to mind. The *Queen* must have just docked when it happened, because you could still see bony queues, as though they were waiting for customs inspection.

Some of the bags had been opened and the contents scattered around—naturally, somebody was bound to think of looting the *Queen*. But there were as many that hadn't been touched as that had been opened, and the whole thing had the look of an amateur attempt. And that was all to the good, because the fewer persons who had boarded the *Queen* in the decade since it happened, the more chance of our finding it in usable shape.

Amy saw a gangplank still up, and with cries of girlish glee ran aboard.

I plucked at Vern's sleeve. "You," I said. "What's this about what the *Major* won't settle for less than?"

He said: "Aw, Sam, I had to tell her something, didn't I?"

"But what about the Major—"

He said patiently: "You don't understand. It's all part of my plan, see? The Major is the big thing here and he's got a birthday coming up next month. Well, the way I put it to Amy, we'll fix him up with a yacht as a birthday present, see? And, of course, when it's all fixed up and ready to lift anchor—"

I said doubtfully: "That's the hard way, Vern. Why couldn't we just sort of get steam up and take off?"

He shook his head. "*That* is the hard way. This way we get all the help and supplies we need, understand?"

I shrugged. That was the way it was, so what was the use of arguing?

But there was one thing more on my mind. I said: "How come Amy's so interested in making the Major happy?"

Vern chortled. "Jealous, eh?"

"I asked a question!"

"Calm down, boy. It's just that he's in charge of things here so naturally she wants to keep in good with him."

I scowled. "I keep hearing stories about how the Major's chief interest in life is women. You sure she isn't ambitious to be one of them?"

He said: "The reason she wants to keep him happy is so she *won't* be one of them."

The name of the place was Bayonne.

Vern said: "One of them's *got* to have oil, Sam. It *has* to."

"Sure," I said.

"There's no question about it. Look, this is where the tankers came to discharge oil. They'd come in here, pump the oil into the refinery tanks and—"

"Vern," I said. "Let's look, shall we?"

He shrugged, and we hopped off the little outboard motorboat onto a landing stage. The tankers towered over us, rusty and screeching as the waves rubbed them against each other.

There were fifty of them there at least, and we poked around them for hours. The hatches were rusted shut and unmanageable, but you could tell a lot by sniffing. Gasoline odor was out; smell of seaweed and dead fish was out; but the heavy, rank smell of fuel oil, that was what we were sniffing for. Crews had been aboard these ships when the missiles came, and crews were still aboard.

Beyond the two-part superstructures of the tankers, the skyline of New York was visible. I looked up, sweating, and saw the Empire State Building and imagined Amy up there, looking out toward us.

She knew we were here. It was her idea. She had scrounged up a naval engineer, or what she called a naval engineer—he had once been a stoker on a ferryboat. But he claimed he knew what he was talking about when he said the only thing the *Queen* needed to make 'er go was oil. And so we left him aboard to tinker and polish, with a couple of helpers Amy detached from the police force, and we tackled the oil problem.

Which meant Bayonne. Which was where we were.

It had to be a tanker with at least a fair portion of its cargo intact, because the *Queen* was a thirsty creature, drinking fuel not by the shot or gallon but by the ton.

"Saaam! Sam *Dunlap!*"

I looked up, startled. Five ships away, across the U of the mooring, Vern Engdahl was bellowing at me through cupped hands.

"I found it!" he shouted. "Oil, lots of oil! Come look!"

I clasped my hands over my head and looked around. It was a long way around to the tanker Vern was on, hopping from deck to deck, detouring around open stretches.

I shouted: "I'll get the boat!"

He waved and climbed up on the rail of the ship, his feet dangling over, looking supremely happy and pleased with himself. He lit a cigarette, leaned back against the upward sweep of the rail and waited.

It took me a little time to get back to the boat and a little more time than that to get the damn motor started. Vern! "Let's not take that lousy little twelve horse-power, Sam," he'd said reasonably. "The twenty-five's more what we need!" And maybe it was, but none of the motors had been started in most of a decade, and the twenty-five was just that much harder to start now.

I struggled over it, swearing, for twenty minutes or more.

The tanker by whose side we had tied up began to swing toward me as the tide changed to outgoing.

*

For a moment there, I was counting seconds, expecting to have to make a jump for it before the big red steel flank squeezed the little outboard flat against the piles.

But I got it started—just about in time. I squeezed out of the trap with not much more than a yard to spare and threaded my way into open water.

There was a large, threatening sound, like an enormous slow cough.

I rounded the stern of the last tanker between me and open water, and looked into the eye of a fire-breathing dragon.

Vern and his cigarettes! The tanker was loose and ablaze, bearing down on me with the slow drift of the ebbing tide. From the hatches on the forward deck, two fountains of fire spurted up and out, like enormous nostrils spouting flame. The hawsers had been burned through, the ship was adrift, I was in its path—

And so was the frantically splashing figure of Vern Engdahl, trying desperately to swim out of the way in the water before it.

What kept it from blowing up in our faces I will never know, unless it was the pressure in the tanks forcing the flame out; but it didn't. Not just then. Not until I had Engdahl aboard and we were out in the middle of the Hudson, staring back; and then it went up all right, all at once, like a missile or a volcano; and there had been fifty tankers in that one mooring, but there weren't any any more, or not in shape for us to use.

I looked at Engdahl.

He said defensively: "Honest, Sam, I thought it was oil. It *smelled* like oil. How was I to know—"

"Shut up," I said.

He shrugged, injured. "But it's all right, Sam. No fooling. There are plenty of other tankers around. Plenty. Down toward the Amboys, maybe moored out in the channel. There must be. We'll find them."

"No," I said. "*You* will."

And that was all I said, because I am forgiving by nature; but I thought a great deal more.

Surprisingly, though, he did find a tanker with a full load, the very next day.

It became a question of getting the tanker to the *Queen*. I left that part up to Vern, since he claimed to be able to handle it.

It took him two weeks. First it was finding the tanker, then it was locating a tug in shape to move, then it was finding someone to pilot the tug. Then it was waiting for a clear and windless day—because the pilot he found had got all his experience sailing Star boats on Long Island Sound—and then it was easing the tanker out of Newark Bay, into the channel, down to the pier in the North River—

Oh, it was work and no fooling. I enjoyed it very much, because I didn't have to do it.

*

But I had enough to keep me busy at that. I found a man who claimed he used to be a radio engineer. And if he was an engineer, I was Albert Einstein's mother, but at least he knew which end of a soldering iron was hot. There was no need for any great skill, since there weren't going to be very many vessels to communicate with.

Things began to move.

The advantage of a ship like the *Queen*, for our purposes, was that the thing was pretty well automated to start out with. I mean never mind what the seafaring unions required in the way of flesh-and-blood personnel. What it came down to was that one man in the bridge or wheelhouse could pretty well make any part of the ship go or not go.

The engine-room telegraph wasn't hooked up to control the engines, no. But the wiring diagram needed only a few little changes to get the same effect, because where in the original concept a human being would take a look at the repeater down in the engine room, nod wisely, and push a button that would make the engines stop, start, or whatever—why, all we had to do was cut out the middleman, so to speak.

Our genius of the soldering iron replaced flesh and blood with some wiring and, presto, we had centralized engine control.

The steering was even easier. Steering was a matter of electronic control and servomotors to begin with. Windjammers in the old movies might have a man lashed to the wheel whose muscle power turned the rudder, but, believe me, a big superliner doesn't. The rudders weigh as much as any old windjammer ever did from stem to stern; you have to have motors to turn them; and it was only a matter of getting out the old soldering iron again.

By the time we were through, we had every operational facility of the *Queen* hooked up to a single panel on the bridge.

Engdahl showed up with the oil tanker just about the time we got the wiring complete. We rigged up a pump and filled the bunkers till they were topped off full. We guessed, out of hope and ignorance, that there was enough in there to take us half a dozen times around the world at normal cruising speed, and maybe there was. Anyway, it didn't matter, for surely we had enough to take us anywhere we wanted to go, and then there would be more.

We crossed our fingers, turned our ex-ferry-stoker loose, pushed a button—

Smoke came out of the stacks.

The antique screws began to turn over. Astern, a sort of hump of muddy water appeared. The *Queen* quivered underfoot. The mooring hawsers creaked and sang.

"Turn her off!" screamed Engdahl. "She's headed for Times Square!"

Well, that was an exaggeration, but not much of one; and there wasn't any sense in stirring up the bottom mud. I pushed buttons and the screws stopped. I pushed another button, and the big engines quietly shut themselves off, and in a few moments the stacks stopped puffing their black smoke.

The ship was alive.

Solemnly Engdahl and I shook hands. We had the thing licked. All, that is, except for the one small problem of Arthur.

*

The thing about Arthur was they had put him to work.

It was in the power station, just as Amy had said, and Arthur didn't like it. The fact that he didn't like it was a splendid reason for staying away from there, but I let my kind heart overrule my good sense and paid him a visit.

It was way over on the East Side, miles and miles from any civilized area. I borrowed Amy's MG, and borrowed Amy to go with it, and the two of us packed a picnic lunch and set out. There were reports of deer on Avenue A, so I brought a rifle, but we never saw one; and if you want my opinion, those reports were nothing but wishful thinking. I mean if people couldn't survive, how could deer?

We finally threaded our way through the clogged streets and parked in front of the power station.

"There's supposed to be a guard," Amy said doubtfully.

I looked. I looked pretty carefully, because if there was a guard, I wanted to see him. The Major's orders were that vital defense installations—such as the power station, the PX and his own barracks building—were to be guarded against trespassers on a shoot-on-sight basis and I wanted to make sure that the guard knew we were privileged persons, with passes signed by the Major's own hand. But we couldn't find him. So we walked in through the big door, peered around, listened for the sounds of machinery and walked in that direction.

And then we found him; he was sound asleep. Amy, looking indignant, shook him awake.

"Is that how you guard military property?" she scolded. "Don't you know the penalty for sleeping at your post?"

The guard said something irritable and unhappy. I got her off his back with some difficulty, and we located Arthur.

Picture a shiny four-gallon tomato can, with the label stripped off, hanging by wire from the flashing-light panels of an electric computer. That was Arthur. The shiny metal cylinder was his prosthetic tank; the wires were the leads that served him for fingers, ears and mouth; the glittering panel was the control center for the Consolidated Edison Eastside Power Plant No. 1.

"Hi, Arthur," I said, and a sudden ear-splitting thunderous hiss was his way of telling me that he knew I was there.

I didn't know exactly what it was he was trying to say and I didn't want to; fortune spares me few painful moments, and I accept with gratitude the ones it does. The Major's boys hadn't bothered to bring Arthur's typewriter along—I mean who cares what a generator-governor had to offer in the way of conversation?—so all he could do was blow off steam from the distant boilers.

*

Well, not quite all. Light flashed; a bucket conveyor began crashingly to dump loads of coal; and an alarm gong began to pound.

"Please, Arthur," I begged. "Shut up a minute and listen, will you?"

More lights. The gong rapped half a dozen times sharply, and stopped.

I said: "Arthur, you've got to trust Vern and me. We have this thing figured out now. We've got the *Queen Elizabeth*—"

A shattering hiss of steam—meaning delight this time, I thought. Or anyway hoped.

"—and its only a question of time until we can carry out the plan. Vern says to apologize for not looking in on you—" *hiss*—"but he's been busy. And after all, you know it's more important to get everything ready so you can get out of this place, right?"

"Psst," said Amy.

She nodded briefly past my shoulder. I looked, and there was the guard, looking sleepy and surly and definitely suspicious.

I said heartily: "So as soon as I fix it up with the Major, we'll arrange for something better for you. Meanwhile, Arthur, you're doing a capital job and I want you to know that all of us loyal New York citizens and public servants deeply appreciate—"

Thundering crashes, bangs, gongs, hisses, and the scream of a steam whistle he'd found somewhere.

Arthur was mad.

"So long, Arthur," I said, and we got out of there—just barely in time. At the door, we found that Arthur had reversed the coal scoops and a growing mound of it was pouring into the street where we'd left the MG parked. We got the car started just as the heap was beginning to reach the bumpers, and at that the paint would never again be the same.

Oh, yes, he was mad. I could only hope that in the long run he would forgive us, since we were acting for his best interests, after all.

Anyway, I *thought* we were.

*

Still, things worked out pretty well—especially between Amy and me. Engdahl had the theory that she had been dodging the Major so long that *anybody* looked good to her, which was hardly flattering. But she and I were getting along right well.

She said worriedly: "The only thing, Sam, is that, frankly, the Major has just about made up his mind that he wants to marry me—"

"He *is* married!" I yelped.

"Naturally he's married. He's married to—so far—one hundred and nine women. He's been hitting off a marriage a month for a good many years now and, to tell you the truth, I think he's got the habit Anyway, he's got his eye on me."

I demanded jealously: "Has he said anything?"

She picked a sheet of onionskin paper out of her bag and handed it to me. It was marked *Top Secret*, and it really was, because it hadn't gone through his regular office—I knew that because I was his regular office. It was only two lines of text and sloppily typed at that:

Lt. Amy Bankhead will report to HQ at 1700 hours 1 July to carry out orders of the Commanding Officer.

The first of July was only a week away. I handed the orders back to her.

"And the orders of the Commanding Officer will be—" I wanted to know.

She nodded. "You guessed it."

I said: "We'll have to work fast."

*

On the thirtieth of June, we invited the Major to come aboard his palatial new yacht.

"Ah, thank you," he said gratefully. "A surprise? For my birthday? Ah, you loyal members of my command make up for all that I've lost—all of it!" He nearly wept.

I said: "Sir, the pleasure is all ours," and backed out of his presence. What's more, I meant every word.

It was a select party of slightly over a hundred. All of the wives were there, barring twenty or thirty who were in disfavor—still, that left over eighty. The Major brought half a dozen of his favorite officers. His bodyguard and our crew added up to a total of thirty men.

We were set up to feed a hundred and fifty, and to provide liquor for twice that many, so it looked like a nice friendly brawl. I mean we had our radio operator handing out highballs as the guests stepped on board. The Major was touched and delighted; it was exactly the kind of party he liked.

He came up the gangplank with his face one great beaming smile. "Eat! Drink!" he cried. "Ah, and be merry!" He stretched out his hands to Amy, standing by behind the radio op. "For tomorrow we wed," he added, and sentimentally kissed his proposed bride.

I cleared my throat. "How about inspecting the ship, Major?" I interrupted.

"Plenty of time for that, my boy," he said. "Plenty of time for that." But he let go of Amy and looked around him. Well, it was worth looking at. Those Englishmen really knew how to build a luxury liner. God rest them.

The girls began roaming around.

It was a hot day and late afternoon, and the girls began discarding jackets and boleros, and that began to annoy the Major.

"Ah, cover up there!" he ordered one of his wives. "You too there, what's-your-name. Put that blouse back on!"

It gave him something to think about. He was a very jealous man, Amy had said, and when you stop to think about it, a jealous man with a hundred and nine wives to be jealous of really has a job. Anyway, he was busy watching his wives and keeping his military cabinet and his bodyguard busy too, and that made him too busy to notice when I tipped the high sign to Vern and took off.

VI

In Consolidated Edison's big power plant, the guard was friendly.
"I hear the Major's over on your boat, pal. Big doings. Got a lot of
the girls there, hey?"

He bent, sniggering, to look at my pass.

"That's right, pal," I said, and slugged him.

Arthur screamed at me with a shrill blast of steam as I came in. But
only once. I wasn't there for conversation. I began ripping apart his
comfy little home of steel braces and copper wires, and it didn't take
much more than a minute before I had him free. And that was very
fortunate because, although I had tied up the guard, I hadn't done it
very well, and it was just about the time I had Arthur's steel case
tucked under my arm that I heard a yelling and bellowing from down
the stairs.

The guard had got free.

"Keep calm, Arthur!" I ordered sharply. "We'll get out of this,
don't you worry!"

But he wasn't worried, or anyway didn't show it, since he couldn't.
I was the one who was worried. I was up on the second floor of the
plant, in the control center, with only one stairway going down that
I knew about, and that one thoroughly guarded by a man with a
grudge against me. Me, I had Arthur, and no weapon, and I hadn't
a doubt in the world that there were other guards around and that my
friend would have them after me before long.

Problem. I took a deep breath and swallowed and considered
jumping out the window. But it wasn't far enough to the ground.

Feet pounded up the stairs, more than two of them. With Arthur
dragging me down on one side, I hurried, fast as I could, along the
steel galleries that surrounded the biggest boiler. It was a nice choice
of alternatives—if I stayed quiet, they would find me; if I ran, they
would hear me, and then find me.

But ahead there was—what? Something. A flight of stairs, it looked
like, going out and, yes, *up*. Up? But I was already on the second
floor.

"Hey, you!" somebody bellowed from behind me.

I didn't stop to consider. I ran. It wasn't steps, not exactly; it was a chain of coal scoops on a long derrick arm, a moving bucket arrangement for unloading fuel from barges. It did go up, though, and more important it went *out*. The bucket arm was stretched across the clogged roadway below to a loading tower that hung over the water.

If I could get there, I might be able to get down. If I could get down—yes, I could see it; there were three or four mahogany motor launches tied to the foot of the tower.

And nobody around.

I looked over my shoulder, and didn't like what I saw, and scuttled up that chain of enormous buckets like a roach on a washboard, one hand for me and one hand for Arthur.

*

Thank heaven, I had a good lead on my pursuers—I needed it. I was on the bucket chain while they were still almost a city block behind me, along the galleries. I was halfway across the roadway, afraid to look down, before they reached the butt end of the chain.

Clash-clatter. *Clank!* The bucket under me jerked and clattered and nearly threw me into the street. One of those jokers had turned on the conveyor! It was a good trick, all right, but not quite in time. I made a flying jump and I was on the tower.

I didn't stop to thumb my nose at them, but I thought of it.

I was down those steel steps, breathing like a spouting whale, in a minute flat, and jumping out across the concrete, coal-smeared yard toward the moored launches. Quickly enough, I guess, but with nothing at all to spare, because although I hadn't seen anyone there, there was a guard.

He popped out of a doorway, blinking foolishly; and overhead the guards at the conveyor belt were screaming at him. It took him a second to figure out what was going on, and by that time I was in a launch, cast off the rope, kicked it free, and fumbled for the starting button.

It took me several seconds to realize that a rope was required, that in fact there was no button; and by then I was floating yards away, but the pudgy pop-eyed guard was also in a launch, and he didn't have to fumble. He knew. He got his motor started a fraction of a second before me, and there he was, coming at me, set to ram. Or so it looked.

I wrenched at the wheel and brought the boat hard over; but he swerved too, at the last moment, and brought up something that looked a little like a spear and a little like a sickle and turned out to be a boathook. I ducked, just in time. It sizzled over my head as he swung and crashed against the windshield. Hunks of safety glass splashed out over the forward deck, but better that than my head.

Boathooks, hey? I had a boathook too! If he didn't have another weapon, I was perfectly willing to play; I'd been sitting and taking it long enough and I was very much attracted by the idea of fighting back. The guard recovered his balance, swore at me, fought the wheel around and came back.

We both curved out toward the center of the East River in intersecting arcs. We closed. He swung first. I ducked—

And from a crouch, while he was off balance, I caught him in the shoulder with the hook.

He made a mighty splash.

I throttled down the motor long enough to see that he was still conscious.

"*Touché*, buster," I said, and set course for the return trip down around the foot of Manhattan, back toward the *Queen*.

*

It took a while, but that was all right; it gave everybody a nice long time to get plastered. I sneaked aboard, carrying Arthur, and turned him over to Vern. Then I rejoined the Major. He was making an inspection tour of the ship—what he called an inspection, after his fashion.

He peered into the engine rooms and said: "Ah, fine."

He stared at the generators that were turning over and nodded when I explained we needed them for power for lights and everything and said: "Ah, of course."

He opened a couple of stateroom doors at random and said: "Ah, nice."

And he went up on the flying bridge with me and such of his officers as still could walk and said: "Ah."

Then he said in a totally different tone: "What the devil's the matter over there?"

He was staring east through the muggy haze. I saw right away what it was that was bothering him—easy, because I knew where to look. The power plant way over on the East Side was billowing smoke.

"Where's Vern Engdahl? That gadget of his isn't working right!"

"You mean Arthur?"

"I mean that brain in a bottle. It's Engdahl's responsibility, you know!"

Vern came up out of the wheelhouse and cleared his throat. "Major," he said earnestly, "I think there's some trouble over there. Maybe you ought to go look for yourself."

"Trouble?"

"I, uh, hear there've been power failures," Vern said lamely. "Don't you think you ought to inspect it? I mean just in case there's something serious?"

The Major stared at him frostily, and then his mood changed. He took a drink from the glass in his hand, quickly finishing it off.

"Ah," he said, "hell with it. Why spoil a good party? If there are going to be power failures, why, let them be. That's my motto!"

Vern and I looked at each other. He shrugged slightly, meaning, well, we tried. And I shrugged slightly, meaning, what did you expect? And then he glanced upward, meaning, take a look at what's there.

But I didn't really have to look because I heard what it was. In fact, I'd been hearing it for some time. It was the Major's entire air force—two helicopters, swirling around us at an average altitude of a hundred feet or so. They showed up bright against the gathering clouds overhead, and I looked at them with considerable interest—partly because I considered it an even-money bet that one of them would be playing crumple-fender with our stacks, partly because I had an idea that they were not there solely for show.

I said to the Major: "Chief, aren't they coming a little close? I mean it's *your* ship and all, but what if one of them takes a spill into the bridge while you're here?"

He grinned. "They know better," he bragged. "Ah, besides, I want them close. I mean if anything went wrong."

I said, in a tone that showed as much deep hurt as I could manage: "Sir, what could go wrong?"

"Oh, you know." He patted my shoulder limply. "Ah, no offense?" he asked.

I shook my head. "Well," I said, "let's go below."

*

All of it was done carefully, carefully as could be. The only thing was, we forgot about the typewriters. We got everybody, or as near as we could, into the Grand Salon where the food was, and right there on a table at the end of the hall was one of the typewriters clacking away. Vern had rigged them up with rolls of paper instead of sheets, and maybe that was ingenious, but it was also a headache just then. Because the typewriter was banging out:

LEFT FOUR THIRTEEN FOURTEEN AND TWENTYONE BOILERS WITH A FULL HEAD OF STEAM AND THE SAFETY VALVES LOCKED BOY I TELL YOU WHEN THOSE THINGS LET GO YOURE GOING TO HEAR A NOISE THATLL KNOCK YOUR HAT OFF

The Major inquired politely: "Something to do with the ship?"

"Oh, *that*," said Vern. "Yeah. Just a little, uh, something to do with the ship. Say, Major, here's the bar. Real scotch, see? Look at the label!"

The Major glanced at him with faint contempt—well, he'd had the pick of the greatest collection of high-priced liquor stores in the world for ten years, so no wonder. But he allowed Vern to press a drink on him.

And the typewriter kept rattling:

LOOKS LIKE RAIN ANY MINUTE NOW HOO BOY IM GLAD I WONT BE IN THOSE WHIRLYBIRDS WHEN THE STORM STARTS SAY VERN WHY DONT YOU EVER ANSWER ME Q Q ISNT IT ABOUT TIME TO TAKE OFF XXX I MEAN GET UNDER WEIGH Q Q

Some of the "clerks, typists, domestic personnel and others"—that was the way they were listed on the T/O; it was only coincidence that the Major had married them all—were staring at the typewriter.

"Drinks!" Vern called nervously. "Come on, girls! Drinks!"

*

The Major poured himself a stiff shot and asked: "What *is* that thing? A teletype or something?"

"That's right," Vern said, trailing after him as the Major wandered over to inspect it.

I GIVE THOSE BOILERS ABOUT TEN MORE MINUTES SAM WELL WHAT ABOUT IT Q Q READY TO SHOVE OFF Q Q

The Major said, frowning faintly: "Ah, that reminds me of something. Now what is it?"

"More scotch?" Vern cried. "Major, a little more scotch?"

The Major ignored him, scowling. One of the "clerks, typists" said: "Honey, you know what it is? It's like that pross you had, remember? It was on our wedding night, and you'd just got it, and you kept asking it to tell you limericks."

The Major snapped his fingers. "Knew I'd get it," he glowed. Then abruptly he scowled again and turned to face Vern and me. "Say—" he began.

I said weakly: "The boilers."

The Major stared at me, then glanced out the window. "What boilers?" he demanded. "It's just a thunderstorm. Been building up all day. Now what about this? Is that thing—"

But Vern was paying him no attention. "Thunderstorm?" he yelled. "Arthur, you listening? Are the helicopters gone?"

YESYESYES

"Then shove off, Arthur! Shove off!"

The typewriter rattled and slammed madly.

The Major yelled angrily: "Now listen to me, you! I'm asking you a question!"

But we didn't have to answer, because there was a thrumming and a throbbing underfoot, and then one of the "clerks, typists" screamed: "The dock!" She pointed at a porthole. "It's moving!"

*

Well, we got out of there—barely in time. And then it was up to Arthur. We had the whole ship to roam around in and there were plenty of places to hide. They had the whole ship to search. And Arthur was the whole ship.

Because it was Arthur, all right, brought in and hooked up by Vern, attained to his greatest dream and ambition. He was skipper of a superliner, and more than any skipper had ever been—the ship was his body, as the prosthetic tank had never been; the keel his belly, the screws his feet, the engines his heart and lungs, and every moving part that could be hooked into central control his many, many hands.

Search for us? They were lucky they could move at all! Fire Control washed them with salt water hoses, directed by Arthur's brain. Watertight doors, proof against sinking, locked them away from us at Arthur's whim.

The big bull whistle overhead brayed like a clamoring Gabriel, and the ship's bells tinkled and clanged. Arthur backed that enormous ship out of its berth like a racing scull on the Schuylkill. The four giant screws lashed the water into white foam, and then the thin mud they sucked up into tan; and the ship backed, swerved, lashed the water, stopped, and staggered crazily forward.

Arthur brayed at the Statue of Liberty, tooted good-by to Staten Island, feinted a charge at Sandy Hook and really laid back his ears and raced once he got to deep water past the moored lightship.

We were off!

Well, from there on, it was easy. We let Arthur have his fun with the Major and the bodyguards—and by the sodden, whimpering shape they were in when they came out, it must really have been fun for him. There were just the three of us and only Vern and I had guns—but Arthur had the *Queen Elizabeth*, and that put the odds on our side.

We gave the Major a choice: row back to Coney Island—we offered him a boat, free of charge—or come along with us as cabin boy. He cast one dim-eyed look at the hundred and nine "clerks, typists" and at Amy, who would never be the hundred and tenth.

And then he shrugged and, game loser, said: "Ah, why not? I'll come along."

*

And why not, when you come to think of it? I mean ruling a city is nice and all that, but a sea voyage is a refreshing change. And while a hundred and nine to one is a respectable female-male ratio, still it must be wearing; and eighty to thirty isn't so bad, either. At least, I guess that was what was in the Major's mind. I know it was what was in mine.

And I discovered that it was in Amy's, for the first thing she did was to march me over to the typewriter and say: "You've had it, Sam. We'll dispose with the wedding march—just get your friend Arthur here to marry us."

"Arthur?"

"The captain," she said. "We're on the high seas and he's empowered to perform marriages."

Vern looked at me and shrugged, meaning, you asked for this one, boy. And I looked at him and shrugged, meaning, it could be worse.

And indeed it could. We'd got our ship; we'd got our ship's company—because, naturally, there wasn't any use stealing a big ship for just a couple of us. We'd had to manage to get a sizable colony aboard. That was the whole idea.

The world, in fact, was ours. It could have been very much worse indeed, even though Arthur was laughing so hard as he performed the ceremony that he jammed up all his keys.